SeaRISE

SARAH HOLDING

SeaRISE
© Sarah Holding 2014

Published by
Medina Publishing Ltd
310 Ewell Road
Surbiton
Surrey KT6 7AL
United Kingdom
medinapublishing.com

ISBN: 978-1-909339-14-9

Printed and bound by
TJ International Ltd
tjinternational.ltd.uk

printed on environmentally-friendly Munken woodfree FSC certified paper

Thermochromic cover by
LCR Hallcrest Ltd
lcrhallcrest.com

Illustrations by
The author, Nina Holding, Ray Holding and Louis Holding

CIP Data: A catalogue record for this book is available from the British Library.

Sarah Holding asserts her moral right to be identified as the author of this book.

SeaRISE

Book 3 of the
SeaBEAN Trilogy

SARAH HOLDING

Medina Publishing

Contents

HS TERRASTATIC
AMAZON'S HOUS

AROB2007
CCHEE806

VILLAC
HS AIRLOCK

HADRON SERVICES LA

SATELLITE IMAGE
ST. KILDA
08:00, 10.09.2118

Prologue

A solar storm has been raging for months. There is hardly any difference between night and day – the sky is constantly alive with a shimmering brightness, cycling rapidly through a vivid array of colours in the Earth's outer atmosphere. No one calls it the Northern Lights any longer, since the phenomenon can be seen just as clearly at the Equator.

All that can be seen of the small forest in Village Bay on the island of St Kilda, planted by the inhabitants of the 21st century over an 80-year period, are a few scorched and torn upper branches reaching upwards out of the sea like pitiful drowning limbs. The vertical tide marker the islanders installed alongside the jetty 50 years ago when the sea level started to rise rapidly is now completely underwater. At high tide, waves lap the front doorsteps of the arc of cottages long since abandoned, and at low tide their broken windows look out over a salty bog – ideal for wading seabirds, if only they were still around. But their colonies are greatly reduced in size, the birds either dead or departed owing to the ravages of this infernal weather.

There is apparently just one human inhabitant left on this lonely island – a solitary figure with rusty hair wearing breathing apparatus and a long silver coat to protect him from the solar radiation. He emerges like an amphibian from under the sea each day via a hatch beneath the old gun emplacement. Maybe he comes up for air or because, despite the risks, he needs to take readings: air quality, temperature, radiation levels, sea level. Today, he struggles for longer than usual with the hatch, which is slowly rusting over. He hesitates, perhaps concerned that he might not be able to access his subterranean chamber this time if he closes it behind him. Leaving the hatch open, he adjusts his oxygen supply and then begins his slow trudge up to the terrastation on the mountain ridge where his monitoring equipment is stored. Battling against the fierce, hot wind, he puts up the hood of his silver coat and proceeds uphill.

Alice's Blog #1

Monday 27 August 2018, Liverpool

It's so frustrating! If only we could crack the password on Karla Ingermann's laptop and get into its hard drive, then maybe we'd be able to figure out why the C-Bean disappeared like it did three weeks ago when Charlie, Lori and I arrived in Liverpool. We've been trying ever since we got here. Maybe we can't get it to work because it overheated when we were in the C-Bean.

Since we reset the C-Bean one day into the future to avoid being stuck in 1930 forever, Charlie's been convinced Karla was trying to summon the C-Bean remotely. He thinks she's the reason it disappeared right after we arrived, taking Dr Foster and Spix with it. He could be right because I'm sure that's how she escaped from 1918 back to her own time – I mean, by controlling the C-Bean remotely – no one else knows as much as she does about its computer code!

I still have absolutely no idea why Karla would want to capture our old teacher - or our parrot - but it's made me wonder if there is some kind of connection between Karla and Dr Foster that we don't know about. It was when he said 'I want to tell you about Plan B' on the dockside in Liverpool that I got suspicious, because Karla also talked about Plan B in her sleep when we were imprisoned in Lady

Grange's cleit in 1918, and next morning when I asked her what Plan B meant, she got really nasty. So I have a funny feeling there could be something on her hard drive that will explain the link between the two of them, and maybe even tell us what Dr Foster tried to warn me about Plan B and why he thought there was something wrong with the C-Bean.

Anyway, the laptop's our only hope now. Mum took the Mark 3 cardkey away from us the minute she found out that we'd used the C-Bean to get to Liverpool. So now we can't even try to summon it back and see if it's still working.

Wednesday 29th August 2018, Liverpool

Today it's 88 years exactly since my island St Kilda was evacuated in 1930. I'm trying to imagine what it must have felt like to have to leave your home and go and live somewhere on the mainland forever. It's a bit like what's going to happen to me next year when I leave St Kilda to go to my sister Lori's boarding school in Glasgow. Only I'll get to come back home in the holidays. There are only a few days of the summer holidays left and, to be honest, I'd quite like to be back on St Kilda right now – Granny and Gramps' flat is a bit crowded, what with seven Robertsons and Charlie all staying here.

It felt strange getting a postcard from St Kilda this morning. Edie sent it. She wrote on it that she's really looking forward to visiting our new school in Glasgow in October. Mum calls it our 'Induction Programme'. We will be staying in Glasgow in a dormitory for three nights and in the daytime we'll be doing things like experiments in a chemistry lab and acting out a play and stuff. I can't wait to go because they have loads of really cool things we don't have, like a theatre, a library, a swimming pool and a tuck shop.

Friday 31st August 2018, Oban

Last night I had this weird dream that Village Bay was flooded and my baby brother was floating away in his Moses basket and I had to swim and rescue him. Maybe it's because we're getting the ferry back to St Kilda today, or it could be because Charlie and I watched a film called *Noah* yesterday. Except there weren't animals being rescued in my dream. In fact there weren't any animals at all. Or any birds. Just too much water. All I can remember is that I was worrying about rescuing the C-Bean but I knew I had to save Kit first. Because weirdly, even though I know for a fact it floats, the C-Bean was sinking.

I don't know why I told you that. I might not even upload this. I think the dream was just a sign that things feel a bit 'out of sorts', as my Mum puts it. Like when I tried to log back into my blog about St Kilda on Gramp's computer yesterday, the settings had been changed and I couldn't get into it. I've emailed the website administrator but they hadn't replied by the time we left Liverpool. So for now I'm writing my blog in a notebook and I'll type it and try again to upload it when I get back.

We're catching the new super-stormproof ferry from Oban to St Kilda today – it's going to be running every three days from now on all through winter, even when the waves are atrocious. Dad says he's started noticing funny things with the waves out beyond Village Bay where the Evaw wave energy machines are. He says some days there are strange whirlpools in the water instead of long rolling waves and they're getting these weird readings from the monitoring equipment. Plus he's noticed loads of dead sea creatures floating on the surface. Some marine biology experts are coming over from Portugal in a couple of weeks to look into it.

And lastly, I have one other thing to report – Lady Grange is completely well now and she's decided to stay on St Kilda. Mum told me yesterday Lady Grange is going to be her new teaching assistant at school. Apparently, she's going to be teaching us history and handwriting, which makes sense for someone who's from the 18th century and likes writing long letters.

The light inside Alice's globe beside her bed grew brighter and brighter until she half opened her eyes. It was much better than an alarm clock as a way of waking up and, besides, it was her secret reminder of all the places she'd been around the world. Alice scrunched up her pillow and half sat up in bed. She could hear her parents moving around in the kitchen, the clatter of things being put out for Saturday morning breakfast, the odd gurgle from her baby brother Kit, Spex pushing his dog bowl around the flagged floor as he licked it clean.

Alice wriggled in the warmth under her duvet and stared up at the glow-in-the-dark stars on her ceiling. It felt good to have her old bedroom back exactly how it used to be before the fire. And it was good to be back on St Kilda, even if it was the end of the summer holidays. School was starting again on Monday – her last year at their tiny island primary school of six children before she could join her sister Lori at high school on the mainland. Alice was even glad to have her mother back as their teacher again. 2018 had felt very disjointed so far, what with the arrival of baby Kit, and the arrival and departure of Dr Foster, their replacement teacher, followed by the appearance and suspicious disappearance of the C-Bean's designer, Karla Ingermann, quite apart from all the crazy comings and goings they'd had in the C-Bean itself. And now, with Spix gone – apart from their dog Spex – the only character still left on St Kilda from all their time travel adventures was Lady Grange.

It made Alice feel dizzy just thinking about everything that had happened in the last eight months, and she had already decided that, this school year, the past would remain in the past, while Alice herself would remain in the present and wait impatiently for her future to begin, just like any normal 11-year-old kid. Anyway, now that the adults knew about the C-Bean's time-travel function, it was useless thinking they would have any further adventures in their 'rather too mobile classroom', as her dad put it. Her mum – that is to say Mrs Robertson – had been required to write a full report for the Hebridean School Board about what had taken place when Alice, Charlie and Lori vanished the morning they were supposed to leave by ferry for Oban, and then just turned up in Liverpool the next day, apparently in the C-Bean. Alice could scarcely imagine how her mother had managed to explain this particular event, and was grateful for her mum's sake that not everything had come to light – as Alice saw it, apart from James and Donald Ferguson, it was beyond any adult's imagination to grasp the full extent of their time travels.

'Alice, are you getting up now? Breakfast is ready,' her mother called.

'In a minute!' Alice slid sideways out of bed, feeling the strands of her orange shaggy rug tickle between her toes. She stood up, pulled on her dressing gown and shuddered just like Spex when he was shaking off water. Then she took a deep breath, opened the drawer of her bedside cabinet and took out the Mark 3 cardkey that her mum had given back to her, James Ferguson's red notebook and the photo of his christening, together with his letters and Donald's sheaf of wartime memoirs. Alice knew these things all meant a lot to her, but she also realised they were a strange burden she'd been carrying. Even the things that no longer existed still weighed heavily – the other, older, brown notebook that had belonged to James and the Mark 4 cardkey, both destroyed when their house caught fire. This was all that was left.

'Time to move on,' she murmured to herself, pulling an old shoebox from under her bed. She emptied out the random assortment of toys, birthday cards and dead batteries, and placed her historical items inside in a neat pile. She put the lid back on and then, using a black felt-tip pen, wrote in capitals on the lid of the box:

1ST SEPTEMBER 2018
TIME CAPSULE OF ALICE ROBERTSON

It would need a better box, she decided, slipping the pen into her dressing-gown pocket. But she already knew where it should be left – in the secret chamber under the gun emplacement. She slid the box back under the bed, and decided she would perform the ceremony with her schoolmates Edie and Charlie after their first day back at school on Monday.

Early on Monday morning, Alice pushed Kit's buggy slowly along the main street of the Village down to the Burneys' house with Spex running on ahead, thinking he was being taken for a walk. Edie Burney's mother was going to take care of him and Kit during the day from now on, so that Alice's mother could teach the children again.

Alice had an odd feeling, as if she was in several places at once. Except, she realised as they reached the Burneys' front door, they were all the same place – her own village street – but since she'd now walked down it in no fewer than five other periods in time as well as her own – 1851, 1918, 1930, 1944 and 1957 – it had a very peculiar effect on her.

'Spex, sit. Good boy.' She patted his head, but he looked bitterly disappointed that his walk had already come to an abrupt end. Alice knocked on the door, just like she had in the 20th century when it had been Dora's house. Her dad once told her this feeling when you think you've done something or been somewhere before was called 'déjà vu' – he reckoned that although it feels as if something's already happened, it's just your brain playing tricks on you. Except that, for Alice, this was real déjà vu – she had walked through this very same door in 1930, the day they got Spix back. As the door opened, Alice had her eyes half closed and was picturing her bright blue parrot in its cage in Dora's living room. Spex slunk inside the house, tail between his legs. Edie's mum smiled and lifted Kit out of the buggy.

'Come here, my little lamb! Alice, run along now, you'll be late. You look like you're not quite awake yet, sweetheart: did you eat enough breakfast?' Mrs Burney asked.

'I'm fine, thanks. I was just remembering something,' Alice said, turning to leave, one half of her still in 1930.

The class was sitting in silence when she arrived and there was a tense mood hanging over everyone. Alice slid into her seat and darted a quick look at Charlie. He raised his eyebrows in a mock question and nodded towards their teacher, who was engrossed in reading a letter. It had evidently just arrived, since Mr Butterfield was hovering at her elbow as if expecting Mrs Robertson to write an instant reply for him to deliver by return. Alice peered at the papers on her mother's desk, and spied an envelope with the logo of a spinning globe on it. It was from the C-Bean manufacturer and Alice knew immediately it could mean only one thing – Karla.

Mrs Robertson cleared her throat and looked up to address the class. Six pairs of eyes were trained on her face.

'OK, kids, this is how it is. Sorry to be the bearer of bad news, especially on our first day back. Our C-Bean has, as you know, caused some concern among the authorities, and it seems that this has escalated to a very high level now, with the Ministry of Defence getting involved for some reason. The German company that manufactures these education pods have written to say they need to recall the C-Bean for a complete refit, but I've also received another, more serious, letter from the Ministry of Defence, who are sending a Scottish officer over to the island next week, apparently in order to impound the C-Bean and carry out a full enquiry. They say 'suspicious circumstances' have been brought to their attention, and they want 'our complete cooperation'.

Her mother looked up at the row of disappointed faces. The two Sams were simmering with fury and confusion. They kept looking out of the window at their beloved black cube standing innocently in the schoolyard, and then back at each other. In the end, they could not contain themselves.

'But they can't take it away – it's ours!' Sam F blurted out.

'Yes, that's not fair, Mrs Robertson. It was a present!' chimed Sam J.

'I know, I know, but I don't think they will let us keep it, boys, I'm sorry. Not now. Not after what's happened.'

Alice felt sure that the suspicious circumstances they'd mentioned had nothing to do with the excursion to Liverpool and probably had more to do with Karla disappearing and not being who she said she was, and who knows what else. It seemed to Alice that it would be better if the Scottish officer took the C-Bean away than if it was returned to Karla's company. That is, if it even belonged to them.

Edie put up her hand.

'Can we still have lessons in the C-Bean until it's taken away, Mrs Robertson?'

'I'm not sure. It doesn't say anywhere in the letter that we shouldn't use it in the meantime ...' Mrs Robertson's voice trailed off with uncertainty. Charlie had the look of someone with a light bulb switching on above his head.

'Well, if it's going to be taken away from us, we should at least have a final goodbye celebration – how about we have a sleepover in it, like they do at the Science Museum in London sometimes, you know, with our sleeping bags?' he suggested casually, except that Alice could hear the sense of urgency in his voice – she'd heard it before.

Mrs Robertson glanced up at Mr Butterfield, then at Lady Grange who was sharpening pencils beside her, and shrugged her shoulders.

'Great idea – why not, Charlie? You can all do that on Friday evening, if you like. Now let's get on with some work, shall we?'

Mr Butterfield tugged one end of his moustache for a moment, and then said 'Right, that's sorted then. I'll be off, Jen – got to do my "mailboat" duties.'

'Mailboat,' Alice murmured, picturing all those messages people used to send in the olden days from St Kilda in strange little home-made packages, all sealed up to float across the sea like messages in a bottle, hoping for food, medicine or salvation. She thought about how she'd sent her own messages back and forth in time to James using the 'instant mailboat' drawer on his prototype C-Bean. If only she could send some kind of mailboat now, to appeal for the C-Bean's salvation or, at the very least, to stop it from being taken away.

Alice's Blog #2

Monday 3rd September 2018

I can't believe they're taking away our C-Bean. It's the worst news ever.

After school today we all went back to Charlie's house to talk about it and try to think of way to stop them, but no one came up with anything. We ended up just arguing about my Time Capsule idea. Charlie and Sam F both wanted to put a load of other stuff in it, so people in the future would know something about our life in 2018, like that we eat etc. Edie thought it was stupid and said the food would go off, but Charlie insisted it was worth it. So we raided his mum's kitchen cupboards and decided to put a jar of Scottish honey, a packet of rice, some teabags and a tin of baked beans in the capsule. Hannah wants to put in some drawings she's done of all the lovely nature on St Kilda, you know, birds and flowers and mountains and stuff. I can't decide what I want to put inside. Sam F and Sam J want people in the future to know what technology looked like in 2018 so Sam F put in his walkie-talkie set and Sam J added his wind-up torch. Edie said she wasn't going to put anything in because it was a silly idea, so to annoy her Charlie added a pair of pink plastic chopsticks he'd been given and said 'If you think that's silly Edie, it's so they can eat the rice'.

Edie started to sulk then so Charlie went to ask his dad for a better time capsule box. He came back with this sturdy metal container with a complicated catch that the army left behind in one of the old huts they've just demolished. It has a label on one side that says 'War Office Property'. When I saw that, I realized James used a box just like it to make the instant mailboat drawer on his prototype C-Bean.

Charlie's dad came to see what we wanted the box for. We asked him how long a time capsule should be left until it gets opened, and he reckoned a hundred years is about the right amount of time. He told us that when he was a little boy growing up in Hong Kong they'd found a box like ours in his neighbourhood when they were digging the foundations for a new skyscraper. The box had been buried in 1880 and had some very interesting Victorian items in it that are now in the Hong Kong Museum.

Just before we closed up our time capsule for the last time, I told the others to wait. I suddenly knew what I wanted to put inside it: my hamburger seabean from the nature table at school. That'll be something very interesting for someone to find a hundred years from now and put in a museum, especially if as Dad says the ocean currents have all changed by then and seabeans aren't getting washed up here any more. Maybe there won't even be seabeans in a hundred years' time if we carry on cutting down the rainforest – the trees they grow on won't even exist, so people in the future won't have ever seen one.

Both the Sams said it would be epic if we threw our time capsule off the top of the cliffs, but nobody else agreed. We had another long argument and in the end Edie and Hannah agreed with Charlie and me that we should leave it in the underground chamber under the gun emplacement. So we hid it under a pile of stones in one corner of the chamber. Charlie thinks that one day in the future an archaeologist will find it.

A fter tea on Friday evening the children returned to the schoolyard in their dressing gowns and pyjamas. Lady Grange was on hand to supervise laying out their beds for the night inside the C-Bean.

'This is too much! Why did you bring so many of your belongings, children?' she fretted, as they piled into the C-Bean with their pillows, sleeping bags, snacks, books, pens, teddies and electronic gadgets (including Karla's laptop, because Charlie thought that bringing it inside the C-Bean might allow them to get around the password issue somehow). The last to enter the pod was their class pet, Spex, who already had his beady eye on the bag of food.

'Looks like you've brought enough midnight snacks to sink a battleship,' Mrs Robertson remarked when she arrived, having put Alice's brother Kit to bed.

'But not enough to sink a C-Bean,' Charlie joked back.

'So listen up, kids. Seriously, there's to be no funny business tonight, do you understand? No getting the C-Bean to take you to any foreign places and especially no getting it to move you forwards – or backwards, for that matter –

in time. We don't want a repeat of The Liverpool Incident, do we, Alice?' Mrs Robertson looked pointedly at her daughter.

'Mum, it's just a sleepover, OK? We won't do anything. Promise!' Alice protested.

'Right, I'll leave you to it, then. Don't eat too many sweets or you'll never get to sleep. I'm putting Charlie in charge of lights out, as he's the oldest,' Jen Robertson said.

'Well, technically that's Alice's job, Mrs Robertson. The C-Bean doesn't usually obey my commands.'

'OK, Alice. No later than ten o'clock, then.'

Alice looked at her watch and nodded. It was almost nine o'clock.

'But we've got to have our midnight feast at midnight, Mrs R!'

'That's why it's called a midnight feast!' the two Sams implored.

Their teacher raised her eyebrows for a moment, then laughed and shook her head.

'OK, I'm off. Lady Grange will tuck you in.'

Lady Grange bid them all goodnight by muttering a little blessing, starting with the eldest.

'Hannah, are you feeling unwell? You are very quiet,' she observed when she came to the youngest.

'She's fine, aren't you Hannah?' Edie nudged her sister, who was drawing something on her iPad.

Finally Hannah spoke: 'Lady Grange, what do we do if we need to go to the toilet in the night?'

'The school is not locked, my dear, and I will leave a candle burning, so you can go inside to visit the – what is it you call it – the "loo"? Goodnight, dear children.' Lady Grange smiled and blew them all kisses, then stepped out of the C-Bean and gently closed the door behind her.

There was a bit of an argument about who was going to sleep next to whom, but when the C-Bean started to make the floor go all springy and fluffy no one seemed to mind anymore where they slept. They bounced around for a bit, with Spex barking in excitement, until Sam J spilled his drink and Sam F complained he'd got crumbs in his sleeping bag, and then things settled down.

'Erm … so, guys, what now?' Charlie asked in an exploratory tone.

'What do you mean, "what now", Charlie? We're just going to sleep, right? No funny business, remember?' Edie said testily.

'OK, whatever,' Charlie said, rolling his eyes.

'What about some stories?' Sam J asked.

'Good idea,' replied Alice, and thought for a second.

'Well, since we can't go on any actual adventures this evening, how about we listen to *The Time Machine* by H. G. Wells?' she suggested, remembering that Donald Ferguson had told her it was his favourite book.

'OK, that sounds cool,' replied Sam J, zipping up his sleeping bag and settling back into his pillow. The C-Bean's walls dimmed to a cosy glow and a voice began:

The Time Traveller (for so it will be convenient to speak of him) was expounding a recondite matter to us. His grey eyes shone and twinkled, and his usually pale face was flushed and animated. The fire burned brightly, and the soft radiance of the incandescent lights in the lilies of silver caught the bubbles that flashed and passed in our glasses…

The C-Bean's walls were flickering to suggest the flames from the fire, and images of what Alice supposed were the 'lilies of silver' waved in the firelight. The storyteller's voice sounded exactly like Donald's and Alice found herself counting how many children there were in the C-Bean just to check if he was among them. But there were still just six of them. She pictured the Time Traveller in ragged black clothes, like Old Jim. The voice continued, but after a short while Alice realised she was struggling to give it her full attention, because half of her was drowning in a flood of vivid memories brought on by being back inside the C-Bean.

You must follow me carefully. I shall have to controvert one or two ideas that are almost universally accepted. The geometry, for instance, they taught you at school is founded on a misconception.'

'Isn't that rather a large thing to expect us to begin upon?' said Filby, an argumentative person with red hair.

Sam F butted in, and the C-Bean immediately paused its narrative.

'This sounds really boring, Alice. Do we have to listen? Can't we play a game instead?'

Given his red hair, Alice was vaguely imagining a grown-up version of Kit playing the part of Filby and questioning how time travel worked. She began asking herself whether some of the things she'd been taught were also untrue.

'You don't have to listen if you don't want to, Sam,' she said dreamily, stroking Spex's head. 'Go on …' she urged the C-Bean.

'… Nor, having only length, breadth, and thickness, can a cube have a real existence.'

'There I object,' said Filby. 'Of course a solid body may exist. All real things –'

'So most people think. But wait a moment. Can an instantaneous cube exist?'

'Don't follow you,' said Filby.

'Can a cube that does not last for any time at all, have a real existence?'

'Is this a story about our C-Bean, Alice?' Hannah asked.

'Sort of…' Alice was already half asleep, and couldn't tell or care anymore if she was hearing the story or making it up. Did their cube really exist? When she made it vanish, did the C-Bean no longer exist in space and time? And, if that was so, would there be anything 'left' for the Ministry of Defence to take away?

The Time Traveller continued,

Time is only a kind of Space. Here is a popular scientific diagram, a weather record. This line I trace with my finger shows the movement of the barometer. Yesterday it was so high, yesterday night it fell, then this morning it rose again, and so gently upward to here. Surely the mercury did not trace this line...

In her mind's eye, Alice was picturing an old man poring over weather records, his wrinkled fingers following a line of liquid mercury that trickled across diagrams and rows of figures. It reminded her of the rivulets of mercury they'd seen in the muddy tyre tracks at the gold mine in Brazil and the contents of the mercury cylinder they'd brought back from Hong Kong. The last thing Alice heard before sleep took over was:

The Time Traveller smiled round at us. Then, still smiling faintly, and with his hands deep in his trousers pockets, he walked slowly out of the room, and we heard his slippers shuffling down the long passage to his laboratory...

Alice was woken by Hannah shaking her shoulder.

'Alice, I need to go to the toilet, but I can't get out – the C-Bean's door won't open. Can you make it open for me?'

The interior of the C-Bean was in darkness, full of the sounds of sleeping children and the occasional whimper from the dog. Alice focused her eyes on the luminous hands on her watch – 00.03. So much for their midnight feast!

'OK, just a minute,' Alice whispered, easing herself out of her sleeping bag, trying not to disturb Edie lying next to her. She crept around the edge of the C-Bean to the side where the door was, and breathed the command 'Open'.

Nothing happened. She tried using the 'goodbye' command instead, issuing it a little louder. They both waited, listening. There were clanking sounds outside. It sounded like Mr McLintock was in the schoolyard for some reason, reeling in the thick tow chain on the back of his pick-up truck.

Something clanged against the roof of the C-Bean, and there it was again, the tow chain noise. This time it was unmistakably the sound of winching, a chain being pulled up one link at a time, clink-clink-clink. The C-Bean shifted and swayed slightly, and there was a sudden airborne sensation, like it was being lifted up. It occurred to Alice with a sudden kick of horror in the pit of her stomach that the Ministry of Defence people had already come to take the C-Bean away without realising there were children inside. The others were all waking now, brought round by the lurching motion.

'Is there an earthquake?' Sam F asked drowsily.

'Charlie, Edie, wake up,' Alice hissed, 'something weird is happening.' She felt Hannah's hand creep into hers and grip tight.

The C-Bean, like the children, seemed to rouse itself and slowly come to its senses – the floor hardened over, and the walls grew brighter. And brighter, and brighter.

'That's actually hurting my eyes now,' said Charlie, shielding his face with his hands.

'It's not my eyes – it's my ears that are hurting!' Alice replied, grimacing with pain.

'Me too,' said Edie, her face wracked with worry.

The others just stared blearily, only half awake.

'What's that whooshing noise?' Sam J asked. 'It sounds like a fireman's hose.'

'Sounds like our camping kettle when it's just about to boil,' mumbled Sam F.

Right on cue, the kettle sound became an excruciating whistle that made all the children clap their hands instantly to their ears. Spex started to howl in pain. The whistle turned into a long penetrating wail that gradually petered out into a pathetic whine.

'Who's outside making that noise?' Sam F moaned.

'It's not outside, Sam. The C-Bean's making that noise,' Alice murmured.
'Like it's crying,' whispered Hannah.

They all fell silent, squinting at each other, blank and motionless.

Through the glare, Alice noticed out of the corner of her eye a dark line appearing low down around the perimeter of the C-Bean's walls. She watched as the line rose slowly up the walls, like a blackout blind being pulled upwards, changing the blinding white walls into a deep murky grey. After a few seconds they were enveloped in the dark grey, instinctively turning their faces to the ceiling as it closed over their heads. They were all holding their breath. It suddenly felt suffocating inside the C-Bean. Hannah burst into tears.

Alice remembered how claustrophobic Karla got inside the C-Bean and for the first time understood what it felt like. It was a sort of crushing, hemmed in sensation that made it hard to breathe. Was the C-Bean malfunctioning for some reason? Had they done something to affect its settings? Alice recalled once again what Dr Foster had said just before he disappeared: 'There's something wrong with the C-Bean...'

'We've all got to get out. Now! Something's not right!' Alice cried.

She felt as if she was tumbling head over heels in the air, but her body was standing still. The tumbling feeling seemed to conjure up images that started to whirl out of the grey walls on all four sides, like dark matter hurtling towards them. Alice noticed they were actually images of countless catastrophes – tsunamis, earthquakes, hurricanes, solar storms and raging bush fires, leaving scenes of human and natural devastation in their wake as they washed past. The children, still holding their breath, stared at scenes of people anxiously fleeing with tiny bundles of belongings, or sitting in bedraggled huddles on boats amongst floating detritus as their flooded cities were washed away around them, people fighting over an air-dropped delivery of food, and running in vain from some huge, cresting wave that was about to overwhelm them.

Just as it was all getting too much, the C-Bean switched to a different sequence of images, this time showing cities by night where all the streetlights and the lights inside buildings were gradually being extinguished. By the end, the whole planet was shrouded in a bleak and mysterious darkness. It looked so final that it seemed as though the Earth was about to stop rotating on its axis.

'Look!' Charlie said in a choked voice, pointing at one wall. A clock was ticking away, bright green numbers racing through the decades. Alice watched as it passed from 2050 to 2110 in less than half a minute, the numbers finally slowing – 2111, 2112, 2113, 2114...

'It's predicting the future, right?' she murmured breathlessly.

At 2118 the clock froze and the walls went blank again. An eerie silence hung in the air, although Alice could still feel a ringing in her ears. There was a slight motion to the C-Bean, as if it was shaking after all its exertions.

Then a female voice intoned a routine message that seemed at first quite familiar to the St Kildan children, because it sounded like a shipping forecast. But as they listened, Alice realised it was actually a series of dire environmental warnings.

OXYGENATION 19%, FALLING. AIR QUALITY: POOR, FALLING. MEAN SEA LEVEL: +5M, RISING. MEAN SURFACE TEMPERATURE: 30 DEGREES CENTIGRADE, RISING. RISK OF SOLAR RADIATION: CRITICAL.

There was a pause, and then a male voice added:

REMOTE OVERRIDE COMMENCING.
LEVEL OF ALERT: CODE 9.

The report ended and clicked off. Charlie smirked grimly at Alice.

'Do you still want to get out? Doesn't sound too nice out there in 2118.'

'I feel dizzy,' said Hannah.

'Me too, Hannah, me too,' Alice whispered.

The awful whooshing, whistling noise had started up again. Their centre of gravity shifted and it felt as if the C-Bean was being plunged down into deep water. Alice could feel the pressure building in her ears and the sound of a clanking chain outside, like before. Suddenly it seemed to stop and the C-Bean was yanked violently back up again. The children all toppled over and landed in a sprawling heap on the floor in amongst their belongings. The winching sound continued for another few minutes. Then the C-Bean blacked out.

The children stood up in the darkness and felt for each other's hands and waited, too afraid to speak. Alice started to hum the Scottish sea shanty that had brought the C-Bean back to its senses once before, this time more in an effort to calm its occupants than to restore the machine itself. The C-Bean did something in response that seemed to Alice as if it was taking a register – it started to scan each child in turn, producing a 3D hologram replica of them, appearing one by one like ghosts out of the darkness, their names hovering in luminous green capitals above each holographic head: EDITH BURNEY, HANNAH BURNEY, CHARLIE CHEUNG, SAMUEL FITZPATRICK, SAMUEL JACKSON, ALICE ROBERTSON. It then added, in smaller letters below the names, their dates of birth and other information about each of them: height, weight, eye colour, hair colour and blood type. It then scanned Spex too, and above his hologram it said 'CANINE OF UNKNOWN ORIGIN'. Alice remembered how, the first time she went inside, the C-Bean had scanned her as part of getting to know her, but this time the process felt altogether more hostile and officious, as if they were being treated as criminals and it was collecting evidence about them. For the first time, Alice had a nasty feeling the C-Bean was betraying her for some reason. Was it because it was being controlled remotely again?

When the data collection process was complete, one wall of the C-Bean flickered on to show a framed image that looked like a television screen, and a man with scruffy reddish hair wearing slippers and a white lab coat appeared. Alice guessed he was about 50 years old. There was something a tiny bit familiar about him, but she couldn't work out why. He frowned into the camera as he tried to adjust something on a hand-held device.

'Are you sure it's in remote override mode now? How do I know? Oh, I see. Right.'

The man looked up and cleared his throat to speak.

'ATTENTION PLEASE. THIS C-BEAN MARK 4 HAS BEEN RECALLED ON THE GROUNDS OF SERIOUS MISCONDUCT. THE SIX OF YOU ARE BEING HELD ON SUSPICION OF MALICIOUS DAMAGE TO THE NATURAL COURSE OF EVENTS AND WILFUL MANIPULATION OF STATUTORY TIME. UNDER PRESENT LAW, THIS CARRIES THE HARSHEST PENALTY: TS100. FOR NOW, YOU ARE TO BE DETAINED INDEFINITELY WITHIN THE DEVICE ITSELF, PENDING OUR INVESTIGATIONS. YOU WILL BE INTERROGATED IN TURN. FOOD, WATER AND MINIMAL OXYGEN LEVELS WILL BE MAINTAINED, BUT YOU ARE FORBIDDEN TO SPEAK TO ONE ANOTHER OR TO COMMUNICATE IN ANY WAY. THE PUNISHMENT FOR ATTEMPTING TO COMMUNICATE IS

SOLITARY DE-CONFINEMENT IN SK ZONE 1, WHERE YOU FACE THE RISK OF SOLAR RADIATION, MALNUTRITION, DEHYDRATION AND CERTAIN DEATH. YOU HAVE BEEN WARNED ...'

The screen image flicked off, and a stack of six cardboard trays appeared in a portal in the wall, each with a water bottle, a small paper cup containing three or four coloured tablets and, in an open disposable carton, a portion of brownish food that smelled disgusting and looked like the sort of puréed mush baby Kit would eat.

'Yuck! Spex can have mine – I'm not eating that!' Sam K said, horrified.

'I think the catering options are the least of our worries, mate,' Charlie muttered, scooping out a mouthful with his finger to taste. 'Mmm, worse than eating durian.'

'Shh, we're not supposed to talk, remember,' Edie said, her finger across her lips.

Charlie pulled his mobile phone out of his dressing-gown pocket to check for a signal. He showed Alice, wordlessly pointing at the screen – there was no 5G, but it had detected something called 'Hadronet' and the pointer on the map app indicated they were still on St Kilda. Alice looked at him and shrugged. It certainly felt like they had been transported somewhere else, but maybe they'd just imagined it. She was feeling very sleepy and could hardly even remember what had just happened, perhaps because there was already not quite enough oxygen for all of them.

Fearing the consequences of not eating what they'd been given, the children each took a tray and sat cross-legged on the floor, grimacing as they ate the revolting rations. Sam K managed one mouthful before shoving his tray towards Spex, who gratefully ate the rest. Charlie pointed at the tablets and looked at the others as if to ask what are these for?

'THAT IS YOUR DAILY MANDATORY DOSE OF VITAMIN PILLS, POLLUTION INHIBITORS AND HEADACHE TABLETS, CHARLIE. YOU MUST SWALLOW THEM WITH EVERY MEAL.'

The voice sounded as if the person was in the C-Bean with them, which made all the children jump and turn round. But there was no one there. It was not the man speaking this time, but a quiet female voice with a German accent. Alice knew that voice. She shot Charlie a look and mouthed the word 'Karla' at him.

Edie was collecting their trays and tidying up the C-Bean. She picked up Karla's laptop, nearly dropped it and started blowing the palms of her hands. Alice realised the machine must have started to overheat again. Edie pushed the laptop towards the wall with her toe. The heat from the laptop seemed to activate the C-Bean's scanning function again, because it created a hologram the same size as the laptop, then put up a short description in green capitals floating in space above the 3D image that confirmed Alice's suspicions:

ITEM NUMBER EW9UW9-TOFQFF. PROPERTY OF HADRON SERVICES LIMITED. ASSIGNED TO AGENT KARLA ROBERTSON, BORN LOS ANGELES 2090; USERNAME KROB2090; CHECKED AND ISSUED 1 APRIL 2118, NEXT SERVICE DUE 1 APRIL 2119.

At first Alice thought the information must have been logged incorrectly and that the system had muddled up her name with that of the C-Bean's designer, Karla Ingermann, until she remembered that KROB2090 had been the username of whoever had previously tried to recall the C-Bean when they were stuck inside it, trying to get from 1930 back to the present. So it was Karla, just as they suspected – but why had she chosen to use Alice's surname? Was the spy trying to assume her identity? Alice could not work it out, nor could she understand Karla's connection to Hadron Services. The names Hadron and Hadronet rolled repeatedly round in her head as Alice tried to piece the bits of information together despite her thumping headache. She swallowed her headache tablet and looked across at Charlie, who was leaning against one wall, also lost in thought, his fingers pressed against his temples. He looked up and mouthed the word 'hadron' to Alice, and then started making the shape of a circle with his hand, looping round and round, speeding up the motion as he did so while mouthing what Alice thought were the words 'particle accelerator'.

The woman's voice that sounded like Karla started again.

'COMMANDER HADRON HAS ADVISED ME THAT NOT ONLY WILL EACH OF YOU BE SUBJECTED TO AN INDIVIDUAL INTERROGATION BUT YOU WILL ALSO BE REQUIRED TO PERFORM CERTAIN DUTIES. YOUR FULL COOPERATION IS REQUIRED. WE WILL START WITH THE ELDEST. WHEN YOUR INTERROGATION COMMENCES, THEN AND ONLY THEN, WILL YOU BE ALLOWED TO SPEAK. THIS WAY, CHARLIE.'

None of the children had noticed but, while the woman was speaking, the C-Bean's walls had become cloudy and porous, and when Alice peered into the mist she could just make out a long curving grey corridor. Spex was sniffing the ground cautiously. He looked like he was about to run off into the mist when a bright red canine-looking droid with flashing eyes appeared and issued a crisp and authoritative bark. Spex slunk back and cowered behind Alice's legs. The droid's head rotated through 360 degrees as it assessed the new arrivals and then it suddenly did something that shocked them all – it selected Charlie by firing a tiny dart into his arm. Alice could see a small bead of blood forming on his skin. A fine nylon thread now

joined the robot to Charlie, like a fishing line. He grimaced and clutched his arm in alarm as the droid started to move along the corridor, forcing the poor boy to follow. The children watched as Charlie, slightly unsteady on his feet due to whatever the dart had injected into him, disappeared out of sight – or rather until they realised the walls of the C-Bean had misted up and hardened over again.

After he'd gone, despite there being one person fewer in the pod, it suddenly felt more confined and airless than ever. There was also a sort of smell that reminded Alice of the anaesthetic gas they had given her when she went to have her head injury checked at Glasgow hospital.

'One, two, three, four…' she murmured, looking round and watching as, one by one, Edie, Hannah, Sam J and Sam F all passed out. She was trying to count to ten, but she could feel herself collapsing under her own weight, and realised they had all been drugged.

Alice's Blog #3

Sunday 9th September 2018 (or should that say 2118?)

We've been trapped inside the C-Bean now for more than 48 hours. Yesterday we were all drugged and Charlie was taken for questioning and has not come back. We're all really worried about him. I can only hope he did what Commander Hadron said, and it's just a matter of time before he comes back. If it wasn't for my watch it would be impossible to keep track of time because there are no windows and no connection to the outside world in the C-Bean, and even though our meals seem to arrive at regular intervals, they all look and taste the same so you have no idea whether it's breakfast, lunch or dinner.

It helps me to keep track of time if I write things down as they happen in my notebook. And anyway, there's not much else to do inside the C-Bean anymore except read or play on our digital tablets, because the C-Bean doesn't interact with us or want to teach us things like it used to. Instead it keeps going through loads of information about what's been happening for the last hundred years since 2018. I watched it all at first, but it's too much to take in. I don't want to sound depressing, but the future doesn't really look that good – everything that's still on dry land seems to have been used up or ruined, and everything else is basically flooded. I mean, the sea has risen loads and, from all the satellite images of Earth the C-Bean has been going through, countries like Holland and Denmark and Bangladesh are completely underwater now. I have no idea what that means for St Kilda – the one place it hasn't given us any information about is where we actually are. At least, that's where we think we are but, until Charlie comes back, we don't even know that for sure.

I can tell the boys and Hannah are feeling homesick, and I've tried to get the C-Bean to cheer them up by requesting some nice things to eat, or something to watch, like their favourite cartoon, but it just won't take any notice of me. It's as if I'm no longer the one in charge. And then, to make matters worse, half an hour ago, the person with the German accent who sounds spookily like Karla announced that I'm next to be interrogated. I should have expected it since I'm the next oldest, but Edie is really worried about how she's going to cope with the three younger ones by herself.

I know it sounds awful but I just want to get out of here – the others will be fine without me. I don't care what happens to me – I just want to know where we are, why we're here, and what they've done with Charlie.

Alice was ready when they came for her. She had her trainers on and had taken the precaution of putting her dressing gown on over her red tartan pyjamas, in the hope that when the red droid fired the dart it would not be able to penetrate her skin as it had with Charlie. But, when the droid came to collect her, it swivelled its head and eyed her coldly with its flashing eyes – but for some reason did not attempt to inject her. The moment the walls started to become humid and misty, she stood waiting. Alice was glad of her dressing gown since it was so cold outside the confines of the C-Bean that she could see her breath. The droid made an abrupt noise as if instructing her to follow, then moved off down the corridor. Alice kept her distance, listening to her own footsteps echo off the stainless-steel floor. It sounded like more than one pair of feet. Alice turned to look behind her and, to her relief but also her dismay, saw that Spex was trotting after her, also keeping a safe distance from the droid.

The chilled corridor curved continuously round to the right, lined with smooth silvery-white panels, and was brightly, almost blindingly lit from above. Alice couldn't tell if it was daylight or artificial light. To her left at regular intervals there were pale green doors with circular vision panels that she hardly dared to look into. But she was anxious to know what they'd done with Charlie – what if he was imprisoned in one of the rooms? After she'd passed two or three, she slowed down a little and risked a quick sideways glance into the next one. It looked like an operating theatre, with trolleys of instruments and two people with green masks over their mouths. They were standing opposite each other, bending over a table and opening up what looked like a human head, except inside there was just a load of complicated circuitry. Somewhat unnerved by this, Alice turned to face the other way. To the right there were no doors whatsoever. She passed a thermometer on the wall that indicated it was minus ten degrees centigrade. Alice could already feel the moisture in her nose and eyes frosting over. The droid continued. Alice noticed that it moved by hovering slightly above the ground, making no contact with the floor at all. She could hear that Spex had stopped to sniff something and half turned around, just in time to witness a door slide open and an arm grab the dog. Spex yelped with fright and the door slid shut. Alice hesitated, and immediately a voice intoned from nowhere:

ALICE, LEAVE THE DOG. HE WILL BE TAKEN CARE OF. MOVE ON.

Alice gulped and realised she was breathing more quickly now. She continued along the corridor. She passed a laboratory containing what appeared to be another C-Bean. Several people with white coats and clipboards were standing around testing its invisibility function – Alice momentarily saw the black cube disappear and then reappear. What was this place? Was she inside the factory where they made C-Beans? She felt very anxious all of a sudden. It was as if Spix was squawking inside her head: *Muito mau, perigroso!* Her lips silently translated over and over again: 'Very bad, dangerous!' But this was no time to get upset, Alice realised. She knew she needed to get a grip of herself, so she gritted her teeth and began silently counting her footsteps in order to focus her mind.

A little further down the corridor she almost tripped over the droid, which had pulled up sharply in front of a pair of black-and-gold doors to their right. It was the first time there had been a feature of any kind on the right-hand side of the curving corridor. Alice examined the doors more carefully – the black was darker than the blackest bits of outer space, and across the centre of the doors there was a golden globe protruding from the black. As she moved closer to the door, the globe started spinning rapidly on its axis and it appeared to be lit from within. A whirling stream of letters and numbers like an ancient formula passed across the surface. Alice was just trying to make out what they said when the doors slid apart.

She peered into the dimly lit interior. It was an enormous circular chamber lined with spikes of blue foam projecting from the walls and ceiling. Alice realised she must have been skirting around the outside of this chamber ever since she left the C-Bean. The droid behind her squeaked 'SHOES OFF'.

Alice bent down to remove her trainers, placing them neatly to one side of the entrance, and stepped into the chamber. The floor gave way slightly and she realised that, like the walls, it too was spongy. The droid withdrew and the doors slid shut behind her. Alice was suddenly aware that she could hear nothing. Not a sound. The room was so absolutely quiet that the only thing that made any sound was her own breath. In a strange way it was peaceful after the clattering noise of the metallic corridor, like being inside an enormous soft blue cloud. It was also, she noticed untying her dressing gown, very warm.

Alice padded across the floor through the inky gloom towards the middle of the chamber, where she could just make out a dark looming shape. As she got closer, she could tell it was a C-Bean, and for one moment she felt as if she had somehow been led full circle back to her starting point, until she noticed that this cube was slightly different. The surface looked like it was crawling with tiny insects, all roving over each other in an endless swirling motion, as if the surface material itself was moving around, or was made of countless particles that were constantly rearranging themselves. She reached out to touch it, but her arm passed right through, just like the first time it had passed through the C-Bean's wall when she wrote the coordinates in pen and it transported itself accidentally to Village Bay. But now it was somehow happening in reverse. That time she emerged out of the C-Bean. This time, in a split second, the C-Bean device had managed to envelop her inside itself. The next thing she knew, she was standing in a small room. Except that it wasn't just any old room, Alice realised with a shock – it was her own bedroom.

Alice sat nervously on the edge of her bed, her feet on the orange shaggy rug, looking up in disbelief at the stars glowing softly on the ceiling. Beside her stood the luminous globe on her bedside table. It was spinning on its axis, ever so slowly, just like the hologram on the C-Bean's cardkey and like the globe on the doors she'd just passed through. Alice closed her eyes and shook her head. Maybe she was dreaming all this? But when she opened them again, she was still there. It was a peculiar sensation to be here in her own room – it made her feel both scared and comforted at the same time.

Had the C-Bean conjured up this virtual version of her room from its memory banks? And, if so, how much detail had it recorded? She smoothed her hand over the duvet cover with its printed pattern of grey pebbles. The texture of the cotton felt exactly as she remembered. Alice found herself wondering at what point in time this replica of her room had been made. She slowly knelt down to look under the bed and there in the shadows was the shoebox she'd used as a temporary time capsule. Her heart was beating fast as she pulled it out. There was nothing written on the lid, and it just contained the same junk as it had before – toys, old birthday cards and dead batteries. So the record of this room must have been generated at a time before 1st September 2018, but how long before?

Shaking with nervous anticipation, Alice reached forward and very slowly slid open the drawer of her bedside table to see what was inside. She had butterflies in her stomach, knowing somehow what she would find there.

And there it was – James' old brown notebook, together with the rubbery black Mark 4 cardkey, just where they had been before the fire broke out. She reached into the drawer to grab hold of the precious notebook, but her fingers seemed to move past it and just graze the bottom of the drawer, as if it wasn't really there. Disappointed, she felt around inside the drawer, her fingers apparently moving in and out of the book and the cardkey but not touching them, when suddenly the wall opposite her bed sprang to life with a huge projected version of James' brown notebook, whose scanned pages were slowly turning by themselves.

A shiver passed down Alice's spine. She pulled the duvet off the bed, wrapped it round herself and slumped down onto the shaggy rug beside her bed to watch in awe as James' designs, diagrams and calculations for different C-Bean inventions became animated and three dimensional, emerging out of the screen in front of her as shimmering, mutating forms. Somehow she thought she could hear the sea shanty that she'd sung to her own C-Bean to get it working again. But it was playing so softly that she wondered if she was just imagining it. Luminous green words started appearing alongside a series of 3D design models, explaining the C-Bean's process of invention and organising them into some sort of annotated visual timeline. There was a primitive Mark 1 version with the date '2057–' floating beside it, then a Mark 2 version labelled '2077–' and then she recognised their own Mark 3 version with its illuminated digital keypad and the slot for the hologrammed cardkey. The sequence ended with the Mark 4 version theirs had become. Alice noticed that it had the trademark 'Øbsidon®' floating in space next to it.

Lulled by the music of the sea shanty, she was awash now with weak, untidy memories that had built up inside her like a tidal wave. Immersed in all this information, Alice closed her eyes, struggling to retrieve what she'd once read about Øbsidon in James' notes. She vaguely recalled something about a patent for a material that was being manufactured in China, but frustratingly her mind went blank. She opened her eyes to find that the music and images had vanished. Out of the silence a male voice started speaking in a slow whisper.

'Alice, welcome home. My team has gone to a lot of trouble creating this experience for you. I hope you like it. Make yourself comfortable – climb into your bed if you like – because we need to talk now. It's so nice to see you again. My official name is Commander Hadron, but you know me as someone else.'

The girl woke in a hot, sticky sweat. She had difficulty remembering anything that had happened before she fell asleep, and felt drowsy and sluggish. In fact she was having difficulty simply breathing. She had a dim recollection of a dream about looking for something in her bedroom, and for some reason half expected to find herself there. Maybe she was there – it was too dark to see properly, but she was aware she had her duvet wrapped around her. She struggled to wake properly, and found that she was actually lying on the ground, not in her bed. The ground felt spongy, her hair and clothes were damp with sweat and her arm had gone numb where she'd been lying on it instead of a pillow. It was so hot and airless that she could hardly breathe. Near where she had been lying was a cylinder with straps and a mask attached to it. She thought the label on it said 'XYCEN'. The girl realised she was breathing in short stabs. None of her thoughts would connect together, and the only thoughts that made any sense were about her physical condition – hot, damp, hungry, breathless. Then, above the urgent feeling of hunger, was the realisation that her throat was sore, really sore.

She staggered to her feet, licking her lips and straightening her crumpled limbs. She put on her trainers. A dry, desert wind was whistling through the enclosure, stinging her skin. Despite these external sensations, inside there was still just an empty blank feeling – she had absolutely no idea who she was supposed to be or where. At the same time, she had a nagging sense that she should know these things. A strange orange light was coming from somewhere outside and seemed to be getting brighter. She could read the label on the cylinder clearly now – OXYGEN – and wondered if breathing the oxygen would ease her sore throat. She tentatively put the mask to her face, turned the key on the top of the cylinder as the picture on the mask showed, closed her eyes and breathed in. She had an image that kept flitting through her consciousness of a seething mass of moving particles, none of which she could get hold of. She felt that she needed to latch onto something, anything, to jolt her into remembering. Like this wind – it must be coming from somewhere.

The girl lifted the oxygen cylinder onto her back and slipped her arms through the straps. She turned round until the wind was blowing into her face, inhaled slowly and then walked forwards. After a few steps she banged her forehead on a rough stone lodged in the wall at head height. She reached out and felt the stone, and the one next to it, in fact a whole collection of rough, misshapen rocks that made up the wall through which the wind was blowing. Her eyes were adjusting in the half-light now and, as far as she could tell, the stones went all the way round and over her head. She walked round the perimeter of the stone enclosure, counting her footsteps. The ground was uneven in places. On the fourth or fifth time round, she tripped and half cried out. The sound she'd made tugged at something in her brain – a memory of someone crying in this place. She focused her mind very carefully on the sound of weeping, sniffing – she could picture someone wearing glasses, someone sullen, pale and skinny… and a name: Karla! For a few seconds she simply clung to the recollection of the name alone because, even though she had a partial image of the person it belonged to, she had no idea who 'Karla' was.

'Why is this so hard?' she rasped out loud, her throat laced with pain. 'Am I Karla? I should know who I am!'

She felt her face, but there were no glasses. She felt around on the ground, thinking she could have dropped them, but could not find them anywhere. In all the times she had walked round the stone enclosure she had not looked to see if there was a way out, but she now had an urgent desire to flee from this hot, confined space. Didn't Karla get claustrophobia? Just as this thought surfaced in her mind, another name came to her that seemed in some way associated with this confined and draughty enclosure – Lady Grange.

'Am I Lady Grange?' the girl asked herself, more bewildered than ever. She felt sure she wouldn't be wearing a scruffy old pair of pyjamas if she had such a grand name. She felt in the pocket of her dressing gown for a clue – anything that might remind her of who she was – and found a black felt-tip pen along with a piece of paper on which was written 'HADRON BURN IN HELL'. It was only then that everything fell into place, and she pulled the mask away from her face.

'I am not Karla Ingermann or Lady Grange!' the girl croaked, finally finding the way out of the stone enclosure and shoving the wooden door open with her shoulder.

'My name is Alice, I am eleven years old and I live on a really small island called St Kilda!'

A hot, dry blast of air whipped up to greet her, almost knocking her over. But it was nowhere near as dramatic as the scene that confronted her.

It took Alice a long while to realise that she was looking down into Village Bay. She held the duvet over her head to shield herself from the unbearable heat and drew heavily on the breathing mask. From where she was standing, the whole lower part of the Village was under water. The waves in the bay were rougher and fiercer than she'd ever seen before and, when a wave receded, she briefly caught a glimpse of twigs and sticks protruding from the surface of the seawater. The extent of the flooding was shocking. But it was nothing compared to the raging tempest overhead – the sky was alive with strange sulphurous yellow and orange clouds and billowing flashes of green lightning that made Alice wince.

Things were slowly coming back to her. She felt sure this was some kind of punishment – the term 'Solitary Deconfinement' drifted into her mind, along with the threat of 'SK Zone 1'. In her recollection, there was something dark and ominous attached to both of them, even a hint of death.

With the thought of death uppermost in her mind, Alice remembered St Kilda's little oval graveyard with its crooked old headstones. She looked around and could see the curved stone wall encircling the graveyard in the distance. She headed to where she knew the old entrance gate was. When she reached it, Alice stopped short – gone were the random assortment of gravestones dating from before 1930, each with its name half-obscured by lichen and moss. In their place stood five or six neat rows of translucent blocks, which reminded her of objects she'd once seen sculpted out of ice. She entered the oval graveyard and approached the nearest block, expecting it to feel cool and wet. But, when Alice touched it, she was surprised to find that it wasn't cold at all – in fact it seemed to come to life, showing first an image of the person whose grave it was, and then scrolling through details of their life. As she moved among the rows, each block sprang to life in turn, sensing her presence. At the end of the third row, Alice gasped. The picture on the grave in front of her was a face she recognised instantly – it was her own mother.

Her throat closed up and tears filled her eyes as she read about an event that, as far as Alice was concerned, had not yet happened: Jennifer Robertson, died in Glasgow Hospital in October 2029, leaving two daughters aged 26 and 22 and a son aged 11. Alice was not sure what she felt most upset about – being confronted with the fact of her mother's death, or that there was no mention whatsoever of her dad. Whatever happened in their lives running up to 2029 meant that their family would no longer be together.

Alice couldn't bear to look anymore. She ran out of the graveyard down the hill towards the school, sweat and tears rolling down her face. The grass was boggy and water quickly soaked her trainers and the bottoms of her pyjamas, but she carried on regardless, not even thinking about where she was going or why. She was dimly aware of passing the derelict remains of the old stone houses and seeing strange igloo-like shelters in some of the gaps between the houses. She could hear the wind howling and whimpering in amongst these ruined dwellings, amplifying the hurt inside her. It sounded almost human, this whimpering. Alice had a stitch and stopped for a moment, clutching her side. The whimpering was coming from the house to her left. She stepped inside the doorway to shelter from the fierce wind and crouched down, suddenly exhausted. A voice croaked from the shadows in the far corner of the dwelling.

'Who is there?'

Alice kept very still, afraid that she was so tired she was starting to imagine things. Someone was breathing in short, panicky gasps. There was a pause.

'Alice…' the voice croaked again. It was vaguely familiar. And whoever it was also knew her. Then something seemed to click in her brain.

'Charlie? Is that you?' Alice burbled through the mask, forgetting for a moment she had it on. She rushed over to the corner, where she could see a figure slumped on the ground.

'Oh my God, Charlie! What happened to you?'

Charlie's eyes were rolling in his head, and his lips were dry and crusty and caked in mud. It looked as if he'd been trying to eat soil. Alice noticed his fingernails were black and broken and the ground beside him had scrape marks in it. An oxygen cylinder identical to hers had been tossed aside, presumably because it was now empty. Alice stroked his hair and tried to wipe around his mouth with a corner of her duvet. Then she pressed her oxygen mask to his face and told him to breathe. Charlie's eyes closed and he looked for a moment as if he had passed out, but then he spluttered and sat forwards. The effort of coughing made him open his eyes again – two narrow slits, the whites red and with dark circles on the skin around them. He shivered but managed a limp smile as Alice cuddled up next to him, wrapping her duvet around him.

'Thank goodness I found you! I think we're still on St Kilda, but it's totally different. It's like the climate has changed completely because the village is half under water and the sky is doing weird things. And Charlie, in the graveyard...' Alice bit her lip and failed to finish her sentence.

Charlie tried to lick his lips to speak: 'W –' When he realised he couldn't speak, he made an action that looked like someone drinking.

'Yes, you're right. We desperately need to find water. And food. And more oxygen.'

But neither of them moved. They leaned against each other and in a few moments they had both fallen asleep.

Alice woke for the second time that morning. This time, despite her extreme thirst and hunger and her difficulty breathing, at least she could remember who she was and who she was with. She nudged Charlie awake and helped him to his feet. They were taking turns to breathe the remaining oxygen in the cylinder. A warning light had come on, indicating that there was less than ten minutes' worth remaining.

Without saying a word to each other, Alice led Charlie downhill in the direction of the old wireless station, thinking that there was a slim chance it might contain supplies. But there were bolts and metal shutters on all the doors and windows. They pressed on towards the chapel and the schoolhouse. Alice felt a wave of homesickness wash over her as she stood with her hand on the doorknob to her old classroom. It was unlocked.

The room smelled of mildew and there were strange plants and fungi growing out of what remained of the wooden parquet floor. There were no desks left, but the fireplace was still there, the grate covered in what looked like half a century of dust. Covering one wall, in place of the old maps Alice remembered from Dora's classroom in 1918 and their own project work about the rainforest and Antarctica that adorned the walls in 2018, was some kind of translucent surface similar to the gravestones and the interior walls of the C-Bean. It flickered into life and started showing a presentation entitled

'Two Centuries of Climate Change and Species Extinction'. The images were of Victorian chimneys belching smoke and gridlocked traffic spewing out exhaust fumes. There were maps of the world and graphs dated 1900, 2000 and 2100 showing animal habitats shrinking and growing numbers of animal and plant species becoming extinct. Alice touched the screen gently and another presentation started.

'Charlie, look at this…' Alice whispered. Charlie turned round. The second one began with battle scenes and bombs exploding, and a title came up: 'World War III, 2027–2035'. Alice and Charlie stared at each other in silent disbelief.

Above the sound of the wind outside they could hear a tap dripping.

'Water!'

They both stumbled across the classroom and into the little broom cupboard where Karla used to work and where Dr Foster used to make himself cups of coffee. There was no kettle, no fridge, not even a desk or sink anymore, but attached to the back wall there was still a tap. Charlie cupped his hands under it while Alice tried to turn it on. It was very stiff and in the end it took both of them to force it open. Finally the water came out in a dirty gush of brown liquid.

'Don't drink it, Charlie!' Alice stammered, but he was too thirsty to care. After a few minutes the water ran clear and Alice gratefully slurped some handfuls. They were both soaking wet by the time they'd quenched their thirst, faces wet and shining.

'Better?' Charlie whispered after taking a quick puff of the remaining oxygen.

Alice nodded, her throat soothed by the cold liquid. Whether triggered by being in their old schoolroom or by the running water, she couldn't say, but it was as if a floodgate had opened in her memory. What stuck out in particular was the image of a sturdy metal container.

'Our time capsule, Charlie – we put food inside it, remember? We need to get inside the chamber!'

They found the hatch to the hollowed-out chamber underneath had been left open. The two children peered down into the dark cavern below in a state of trepidation – was it a trap?

'You first,' Charlie hissed.

'Thanks,' grunted Alice, her palms sweating as she clung to the top of the ladder. She realised she had nothing to lose and no choice but to descend and confront whatever awaited them.

After the intense heat above ground, the chamber was pleasantly cool. Alice spied some shiny items stacked against the far wall, next to something else large and circular. She worked her way towards them, and found that the circular object was some kind of metal airlock, with a control keypad numbered '01' next to it. It reminded Alice of the ominous cave with the leaking nuclear warheads and spent nuclear fuel rods she and Charlie had found down here back in the 1950s. She sincerely hoped the airlock wasn't concealing more of the same or, for that matter, something much worse.

'Alice, look over here!'

Charlie found a crate of oxygen cylinders marked '48 Hour Rebreathers'.

They took two out of the crate and helped each other put them on and start the flow of oxygen. It felt good to breathe freely again. Their eyes were slowly getting used to the gloom. Alice looked around her.

'Can you remember where we left the time capsule, Charlie? The stuff inside might still be edible, you never know.'

Without a torch it was difficult to locate the pile of rocks they'd used to hide the box. In the end both Alice and Charlie were crawling on their hands and knees over the slimy cave floor, moving stones aside and feeling underneath for a smooth metal lid. Alice came across something with machine-sealed cellophane edges. Could it be the packet of rice Charlie had put in the time capsule? She fumbled around the same area and felt a long straight ridge. It was the inside rim of the metal time capsule. The lid had been prised open. Other than the packet she'd already retrieved, there was nothing else inside the box. Whoever had raided it had already taken the rest of their items including James' notebook, her hamburger seabean and the C-Bean Mark 3 cardkey. Alice sighed miserably and stuffed the packet into her dressing-gown pocket.

'What have you got there?' Charlie whispered. 'Did you find the box?'

'Yeah, but it's been broken into. They've taken all our stuff.'

'What, all of it?'

Alice felt around once more and came across one half of Sam's walkie-talkie set, but it felt all crusty where the batteries had leaked at some stage.

'More or less, yep. Just a single packet of something.'

'C'mon then, let's not waste any more time down here – let's go.'

Charlie stumbled back over to the ladder where he'd draped Alice's duvet. He pulled the duvet round his neck like a towel and was halfway back up when they heard a male voice shouting above ground.

'Hey you, boy, stop! That's an order!'

Alice froze. Was the order directed at Charlie? She watched as he waited a few seconds before quickly peeping out of the hatch. He immediately hurried back down the ladder, jumped off the last rung and ran over to Alice.

'Quick. Hide. He's coming!' Charlie whispered.

Sure enough, as they crouched in the shadows under the duvet, the man started descending the ladder. Except that he didn't come down the rungs the normal way; he seemed to make his body go stiff and then, holding onto the metal handrail at the side of the ladder, just slid down until his feet touched the floor. Then he turned and marched steadily towards the airlock, as if he could see in the dark exactly where he was going. When he reached the airlock he placed his index finger on the control pad. A tiny bar of light came on, apparently scanning the man's finger. It shed just enough light for Alice to see that the man had curly white hair. A voice spoke.

'Go ahead, Agent AFOS21XV.'

'Code Red. Rudy has escaped again. Request back-up.'

'Back-up declined, Agent AFOS21XV. Leave all flammable items and return to the lab,' the voice droned from a speaker somewhere in the cavern.

The man twitched slightly, fumbled in his pockets for a moment and dropped something, then pressed the control pad again with his index finger. Alice could hear a sucking sound as the airlock opened and a whoosh of freezing cold air together with a shaft of bright light escaped from the exit tunnel on the other side. The Agent entered the tunnel and resealed the door behind him, leaving Alice and Charlie panting with fear in the darkness.

'Who's Rudy? Was it the boy he shouted at?'

'No idea, but I think we need to get away from the village.'

Alice walked towards the ladder, but Charlie went over to the airlock.

'It's this way, Charlie.'

'I want to know what that guy dropped just then.' Charlie was crouching down, feeling the ground around the airlock door. 'Got it,' he said, standing up and brandishing a slim blue cigarette lighter.

'Let's take a couple more oxygen cylinders, just in case,' Alice added.

When they got above ground, Alice examined the packet she'd found in their box. It contained some kind of instant vegetable soup mix. Printed on the cellophane was a use-by date: March 2120. Charlie, meanwhile, was staring in dismay at the flooded expanse in front of him that had once been their village, his shoulders hunched. Alice could hear his stomach rumbling louder than the wind whistling around them. It was hotter than ever.

'My God, Alice – what happened?'

Alice tried to count how many trees there must have been before the flood came. The community said back in 2018 that they were going to plant one tree every year, and it looked like they'd done just that for many years. It was hard to tell exactly how long, because there were gaps here and there where nothing was poking out of the water, but Alice reckoned there were more than 50 rotting away under the sea. She had an image of the submerged forest gradually accumulating in boggy layers of rotting carbon under the sea over millions of years. Like peat.

'I've just thought of a way to light a fire, Charlie – come with me. Let's go back to the broom cupboard, get some water and make some soup.'

'How do we cook it?'

'We light a fire. You've got that lighter thing, remember?'

'But there's nothing to light. All the wood around here is soaked.'

'You'll see.'

They headed off up the village, water lapping their ankles. The tide had now turned and was retreating between the derelict houses, leaving a long line of debris along the middle of Main Street – no seaweed, just a straggly heap of plastic bottles, dead fish, bits of nylon rope, and some empty metal containers. Alice picked up two of them and returned to the tap in the broom cupboard. She rinsed out the containers, filled them with water and took them into the schoolroom, where she stood them beside the old fireplace.

'Right, come with me. I'll need your help.'

Charlie was too weak to protest, and followed meekly behind her, silently breathing into his mask.

Having hunted around for a small rock with a sharp edge, Alice searched inside the cluster of cleitean at the back of the village, well above the tideline. Inside the third cleit she found a patch of peat that was dry and loose, and started to rip small rectangular pieces and hand them to Charlie. They carried back an armful each to the schoolroom, where Alice laid the turfs in the fireplace. At first they struggled to get the fire going with the lighter, using some dry grass as kindling. Eventually, with the containers nestled inside a sort of spongy teepee of burning peat, Alice was happily stirring a brownish vegetable slurry with a twig, waiting for the water to boil.

'Hey, Charlie, do you remember my mum telling us this is how they used to heat our schoolroom in the olden days and how the children took it in turns to bring the peat to school each morning?'

Charlie didn't reply. He was watching the World War III presentation on the wall again and sighing.

'I've been thinking,' Alice continued. 'Assuming it definitely is 2118 and this definitely is St Kilda and we're not stuck in some weird virtual reality computer game, we need to get help. I mean, we need to contact someone on the mainland. I don't think we can trust the people here on St Kilda, since they're the ones who abducted us.'

'How d'you suggest we do that, Alice? Pigeon post? There don't even seem to be any birds left.'

'We'll make a mailboat. Like they did in the olden days. We could use one of the empty oxygen cylinders as the container – I bet they float. We'll put a message inside and seal it up somehow.'

'I s'pose. But didn't they used to take ages to get anywhere? We'll be dead before anyone comes to our rescue.'

'Don't talk like that, Charlie. As long as we stay away from the village and avoid being recaptured, we can concentrate on coming up with a plan to rescue the others and get our C-Bean back. But I reckon we need to make a move before it gets dark – then, if the Agent guy comes looking for that boy who escaped, we won't be around for him to find us.'

'So what's the plan, Alice? I'm too hungry even to think.'

Alice gave the soup a final stir. She tried to pick up one of the containers but it was scalding hot. She thought for a moment and then pulled the tie belt off her dressing gown and, using it like an oven glove, lifted the containers out of the fireplace and handed one to Charlie.

'Here, just eat.'

They both fell silent while the hot broth burned their tongues because they were too hungry to wait for it to cool down.

When their bellies had stopped grumbling, Alice stood up, retied her dressing-gown belt and said, 'Up for a walk now, Charlie?'

'Where are we going?' Charlie asked, following Alice out of the classroom.

'The Amazon's House on the other side of the island in Gleann Mor – if it's still there, that is. We can get some sleep there and then make the mailboat and figure out a plan to rescue the others in the morning,' she puffed as they made their way up to the wall that ran along above the village.

'Who are these "others" you keep talking about?'

Alice turned and looked at Charlie, aghast.

'Well, hello? As in: Edie, Hannah and both Sams. They're still stuck inside the C-Bean where you left us, remember?'

'I don't remember anything... Oh wait, wasn't there a sleepover?'

'Yes, that's when we were taken. During the night. It's how we landed up in this mess in the first place.' Alice carried on walking.

'It's all so hazy. All I remember is some commander guy with red hair asking me loads of questions.'

Alice stopped in her tracks again and turned to face Charlie. It was his mention of the red hair that finally jogged things back into her memory.

'That guy – the one who calls himself Commander Hadron – when I was taken for questioning, it was all pretty creepy. He knew all about me and, what's more, he'd built a complete replica of my bedroom.'

'Weird. What was all that about?'

'I'm not sure, Charlie, but I've got this funny feeling that Commander Hadron is in some way related to me.'

Next morning, while they were assembling the mailboat inside the Amazon's House, Alice had the impression they were being watched. Once when she came to this place, she'd sensed the presence of the ghostly female warrior breathing right next to her inside the dwelling. But this time it felt more real, more human. She could actually feel someone's eyes on her, and kept glancing over her shoulder to check. Alice was about to write a note to go inside the mailboat using the slip of paper and the black felt-tip pen she had in her dressing-gown pocket. As she crossed out the words 'Hadron burn in hell', she not only realised that she must have written them during her interrogation, but also that they were the same words they'd found written in graffiti on the C-Bean when they returned to Central Park in New York. Who was this Commander Hadron and why was he messing with her head? She angrily tore off a scrap of red tartan fabric from the sleeve of her pyjama top and started to attach it to the cylinder so the mailboat would be spotted more easily when it was floating in the sea.

Suddenly a voice spoke.

'I know better Way.'

Alice jumped.

'Who's that?' she mumbled through the rebreather, relieved that her hunch about someone watching was correct, but alarmed all the same.

A skinny boy rolled out of one of the narrow ledges inside the walls of the dwelling. He must have been there all night, but they hadn't noticed.

'Me,' the boy said, standing up and stretching. He was about 14 or 15, Alice guessed, with dark brown skin and almost no hair in places, and was wearing what looked like a faded, slightly ripped, grey wetsuit onesie and neoprene shoes with toes. When he turned to look at her, she noticed that the whites of his eyes were bright yellow. He adjusted a small orange box that was strapped to his arm just above his elbow and then reached into the recess where he'd been sleeping to retrieve a drawstring bag.

'Want eat?' he asked, opening up the bag and taking out a handful of pale green speckled eggs and a coil of rope, which he carefully placed on Alice's duvet. Charlie crept into position behind the boy, his feet planted squarely on the ground, ready for any sign of trouble. Alice was silent. She wasn't sure if this was the same kid they knew had escaped yesterday. The boy carried on regardless, reaching into the bag for another item. This time it was a penknife.

'Not so fast, buddy,' Charlie warned when he saw the first glint of metal.

The boy turned quickly and flicked open the knife. To Alice's amazement, trailing from its handle was a long fluorescent yellow shoelace. It looked exactly like the penknife their teacher Dr Foster had used the first morning he arrived. Alice could picture him now, slitting open the prickly seedpod he'd brought to show them, and all the little seabeans falling out. This unexpected turn of events made her more on edge than ever.

'Charlie, don't move. It's some kind of trap – he must have captured Dr Foster too, if he has his knife!' Alice screeched, pulling away her oxygen mask and pointing at the shoelace. Had this boy made Dr Foster and their parrot Spix disappear in Liverpool? Or was she jumping to conclusions too quickly? Could Dr Foster's penknife still be here on St Kilda simply because he lost it somewhere on the island a century ago and this boy just happened to find it? She stared at the shiny blade. In that case, why wasn't it rusty?

As if reading her mind, the boy quickly flicked the knife shut, stuffed it back in his pocket and grinned toothlessly at her.

'You Prisonbird too?'

'Yes. I mean no. Look, who are you?'

'Rudy,' he said, and held up a grubby hand to high-five Alice. On the palm she could see he'd been branded with an eight-digit code: RBOK2104. Alice's stomach lurched. It was the same format as Karla's username.

Alice looked at her own blank palm, suddenly recalling the strange fortune-teller with all those little Kumulak beans that she'd met in the other St Kilda in Australia. The woman had asked her what she wanted to know the answer to. She still didn't have the answer to her question – she still didn't know why. Why were all these things happening to her? What did it all mean? Alice looked into Rudy's sad yellow eyes, wondering if somehow he was the one with the answer.

'I'm Alice. Are you a prisoner here? Did they capture you from 2018, too?'

'Prison yes. Work in Lab to punish. Four Years. Stole Fishboat. Born 2104. Like Hand say,' he pointed to the numbers.

'So the number is your year of birth…' Alice mused.

'What kind of lab, buddy?' Charlie didn't look convinced, and stood rigidly with his arms folded.

'Hadron Lab. Fix Stuff. Now eat,' Rudy said, sitting down cross-legged on the rough ground. He cracked open one of the eggs, poured the contents expertly into one half of the shell and offered it to Alice. She sat down and took the egg, not sure if she could manage to eat it.

'Like dis,' Rudy said, laughing and tipping the contents of a second egg into his mouth and swallowing. Alice removed her rebreather and did the same, feeling the glop as the yolk passed her throat and headed for her stomach. It had a strange fishy aftertaste.

'Did you collect the eggs yourself? From the cliffs?' Alice asked, wondering if the rips on Rudy's wetsuit were caused by climbing for food.

'Yes. Most Bird die. Too hot now. Few Egg still in Nest. Fall many time. Not like Jutland. Easy-flat there.'

'Jutland? Is that where you come from?'

'Jutland no more. All Water.' Rudy looked forlorn. Then he brightened. 'You want send easy-fast Mailboat? Me knowhow.'

Rudy's offer made Charlie relax a little and he stepped forward. 'Yeah, that's right. You wanna help us, buddy?'

The boy nodded.

'Help me, too. Want get-away. Far. In Blackbox. Like try before.'

'Do you think he means the C-Bean?' Alice whispered in Charlie's ear.

'Maybe. At any rate, he knows stuff,' muttered Charlie. 'Hey, so what's this other way we can send a Mailboat around here, Rudy?'

'Come. Go Terrastation, send Mailboat. Get new Sniff too,' Rudy suggested, pointing at the low oxygen level warning light on Alice's breathing equipment. He picked up his drawstring bag and slung it over his shoulder.

'OK, mate. It's worth a try, but don't try anything funny,' Charlie warned.

The ground was dry and dusty and they kept slipping as they climbed up out of the Gleann Mor side of the island towards the top of the mountain. Charlie led the way with grim, silent determination. Alice left him to his own thoughts and tried to make conversation with Rudy. Despite his really limited English, Alice managed to get out of the boy that his family were rice growers from Jutland, but when he was ten, the sea rose dramatically and he got separated from them. After that, he said, he'd had to survive on his own, and one day he got caught stealing a fishing boat in his hometown – somewhere he called the 'City of Smiles'.

'No Smile now,' he added grimly.

The building Rudy referred to as Terrastation turned out to be a replacement for the radar station near the top of Mullach Mor. It looked quite different from when Alice met James Ferguson there back in 1957. In fact, she decided that this hut looked more like an elaborate bird hide, with its green camouflage pattern printed onto the exterior. Pity there are no birds left to observe, Alice thought to herself.

'Wait, I get in,' Rudy told them.

He pulled something out of a pocket in his grey wetsuit and pressed it on the control keypad beside the door. The door slowly opened. As he shoved the item back into his pocket, Alice caught a glimpse of what he had used to open the door, and recoiled in horror. It was the grubby stump of someone's index finger.

Inside there was some brand-new equipment that looked like it had only just been installed because there was a whole load of discarded packaging lying around and its digital operating manual still sealed. Rudy stood with his hands on his hips admiring the new kit and making appreciative noises for a moment or two. It was obviously not the first time he had forced his way in. He flipped the power switch and a large screen instantly flickered on. He grinned when he read the first thing that appeared on the screen:

```
10.45 HOURS 10/09/2118
@HADRONET ISSUED CODE_RED: @RBOK2104
ESCAPED FROM AIRLOCK 01. @AFOS21XV FAILED TO
INTERCEPT. NB @RBOK2104 UNTAGGED.
```

'Look see!' He was pointing at the word 'untagged' and then pointed at Alice and Charlie and gave them a thumbs-up sign. Charlie peered at the screen and read the message:

'Want untag too?' Rudy proposed.

'How do you know we've been tagged?' Charlie asked warily.

'Look see!' Rudy pointed at two other updates on the screen:

08.00 HOURS 10/09/2118
@HADRONET DETECTED @AROB2007 AWAKE IN
CLEIT85 & @CCHE2006 AWAKE IN HOUSE06

13.30 HOURS 10/09/2118
@HADRONET DETECTED @CCHE2006 & @AROB2007
LIT FIRE IN SKSCH.

'That was us making soup yesterday, Charlie!' Alice whispered nervously. 'Rudy's right – they not only know exactly who we are and when we were born, but where we are and what we're up to out here.'

'I guess. But how and when did we get tagged?'

'Maybe it was when the C-Bean scanned us the day we got taken here, or when we got taken for our interrogation – let's face it, neither of us can remember much about what happened before we found ourselves out here in SK01.'

Rudy walked over to Charlie, took hold of his arm and started to push up his left sleeve.

'Hey, get off me,' moaned Charlie, pulling his arm away. Rudy shrugged his shoulders and let go.

'You want untag, Alice?' Rudy asked, tapping his upper arm.

Alice removed her dressing gown, pulled up what remained of her left sleeve and stared at her arm in alarm.

'Eurghh, what's that? I didn't even know that was there!'

Embedded in her skin just above the elbow on the outside of her arm was a small flesh-coloured rubbery disk that appeared to be covering something. Rudy gently flipped the disk back and underneath was a tiny switch and a hole that looked like a headphone socket. It had a gold rim and was set into Alice's skin. The area around it was red, as though the procedure to fit it had only recently taken place.

'Press Button, count three Minutes. Untag,' Rudy assured her.

Alice held her thumb over the tiny switch, pressed hard and counted slowly to 180. It was excruciatingly painful at first, but after she got past 100, she could feel the pain ease off.

'What's the other thing for, Rudy – you know, the, er… hole?' Charlie asked, peering over Alice's shoulder.

'Is BioPort. For Sniff,' Rudy explained, pulling away the little orange box that he wore on his arm. They could both see the bioport in his arm, and that the orange box had 'O2' printed on the back of it.

'Charlie do untag, I find new Sniff.'

Charlie slowly rolled up his sleeve to inspect his own bioport.

Rudy searched the drawers and cupboards in the hut until he found a long white box with lettering on it that looked like it might contain medicine. Inside was a row of orange units, each one in a protective transparent casing. Rudy removed the casing from one and peeled a sticker off its back to reveal a gold jack plug.

'Ready?' he asked as Alice finished counting. She nodded and Rudy pressed the metal jack plug on the unit into the bioport on her arm. She felt a quick stab of the most unbelievable cold spread through her veins up and down her arm, and then… nothing.

'It only hurts to begin with,' she reassured Charlie, rolling down her sleeve over the unit and putting her dressing gown back on. 'But it's much easier getting oxygen like this than through those rebreathers, that's for sure.'

Rudy handed Charlie another unit and left him to fit it himself. He put the rest of them in his drawstring bag.

'Now we do Mailboat,' Rudy said as he rooted around in another cupboard and produced a small hand-held device shaped just like a giant hamburger seabean. When he opened it up to reveal two hemispherical compartments, Alice first thought that they would simply put a handwritten message inside and float it out to sea, but it soon became clear that it was actually a communications device that used satellite technology and functioned like a very powerful walkie-talkie.

'Think, Alice. Give Instant Message. Right in Brain,' Rudy explained.

'But how does it work?'

'You Instant Alice. Think,' he said again, showing her the band around the middle, which was in actual fact a screen on which a text message could appear.

Alice closed her eyes and focused. The thought that was uppermost in her mind formed into a silent message:

'My name is Alice. I've been taken to 2118 and I'm trying to reach my parents Jen & Mike Robertson to tell them I'm OK.'

When Alice opened her eyes, she saw that the same message she'd uttered in her head was slowly scrolling around the rim of the device in blue. Rudy nodded, as if satisfied with the message.

'Who for Mailboat?' Rudy wanted to know in order to send it.

Alice had been wondering that herself. Who did she know in 2118 that could help them? There was only one person she knew who might be from the future, but she also knew in her heart she was not to be trusted.

'Erm … Karla?' Alice said tentatively.

'You know Namecode?'

'I think it's KROB2090.'

'Hang on a minute, Alice!' Charlie butted in. 'Are you seriously considering letting Karla know we're here? You must be mad!'

'Well, who else do we know that could help us, Charlie? At least she'll know how to get us back to 2018. We're pretty sure she can control the C-Bean remotely. Plus, she did return the Mark 3 to us, remember?'

'Mark 3?' Rudy repeated, pulling something else out of his drawstring bag.

'Like dis?' He pulled out the Mark 3 cardkey and held it up by the corner with a triumphant expression on his face.

'Hey, gimme that. You shouldn't have taken it. It's not yours. What else did you steal from our time capsule?' Charlie tried to snatch the cardkey from Rudy, but he was too quick. In an instant he had Charlie gripped around the chest and was pressing Dr Foster's penknife against his neck.

'Rudy want go Blackbox, want be TS100 like you. We go Airlock 01 now. Back to Lab.'

Alice still had no idea what 'TS100' meant, but she understood from his urgent tone that Rudy was in no mood to be messed with – this was not a suggestion but a command.

'OK, Rudy, easy now. Give me the knife. We'll go and find the C-Bean. Together.' Rudy relaxed his grip slightly and Charlie slid from under his arm and dropped to the floor.

'Charlie, are you OK?' Alice asked as she gently took the penknife from Rudy's hand and closed away the blade. Charlie nodded and stood back up. She instinctively started to sing the sea shanty she used to revive the C-Bean, in an attempt to calm things down. Rudy and Charlie were scowling at each other.

'Rudy, do you know how to make the airlock door open? The one in the underground chamber by the gun?'

Rudy nodded. 'With Deadman Finger' he said matter-of-factly, patting the pocket where he kept it.

'Good, that's settled then. We'll go there now.'

The sky was an angry, seething mass of reds and oranges that afternoon as the three children walked headlong into a fierce hot wind, making their way back down into Village Bay.

'How long has the sky been like this, Rudy?' Alice asked.

'Many Solarstorm. Since few Year. Sometimes 60 degrees C. Many Deadmen. Rudy lucky. Got Solarsuit,' he said stroking the sleeve of his faded grey onesie.

'I see.'

As they approached the gun emplacement, Charlie took the Mark 3 cardkey out of his pocket.

'Hey, look at this, Alice!'

The globe on the cardkey was turning very slowly. As they got closer to the gun, the rotations appeared to be getting faster.

'Hmm. Maybe we will be able to summon it without opening the airlock,' Alice wondered aloud, taking the cardkey from Charlie. 'But let's not do it above ground – we might be seen.'

Rudy was the last to climb down the ladder. He stood in the patch of daylight at the bottom and appeared to hesitate for a moment. Then he took Sam J's torch out of his drawstring bag, handed it back to Charlie and said in a quiet voice 'Rudy sorry. Took Light. Took Rice too. And Chopsticks. Was like Home. Taste nice.'

'That's OK, Rudy, we understand. You were hungry,' Alice said. They all were. She raised her eyebrows at Charlie for support.

'Yeah, no worries, buddy,' Charlie said, but there was not much warmth in his voice.

Alice closed her eyes. She had to get the cardkey to work. She pictured the other children still trapped inside, hungry and frightened. The globe was spinning fast. Charlie flashed Sam's torch beam across the room and Alice thought she could see a flicker of black forming.

'Keep going, Alice.'

She held her breath and concentrated on an image of the black cube, but she couldn't seem to make it appear fully – there was just a fleeting glimpse of it, and then it would disappear. She sang, hummed and talked in a coaxing voice to the C-Bean, but still nothing happened.

'It's not working. The walls of the lab must be too thick for the cardkey to summon it from in there,' Alice muttered finally, disappointed.

Charlie growled with frustration.

'Use Mailboat?' Rudy suggested, getting the device out of his bag.

'Genius. To do what, exactly?' Charlie said sarcastically.

Alice was thinking.

'Wait a minute, Charlie. Karla's laptop is inside the C-Bean.'

'Yes, but it's no good to us there, is it?'

'Can you stop being snotty for one minute and just listen? What if we try to access it remotely using Rudy's Mailboat device? Maybe we could log into it and use it to summon the C-Bean like Karla did.'

'Sounds complicated.' Charlie scuffed his shoe along the ground, kicking rocks. The sound echoed off the ceiling like a clap of thunder.

'Alright,' he muttered eventually.

Rudy handed Alice the Mailboat device and she silently transmitted Karla's namecode into it: 'login KROB2090.'

The reply arrived in her brain almost instantaneously: 'Enter Password'.

'What do you think Karla's password is, Charlie?'

'No idea, Alice. We tried everything already, remember? I'm not a mind-reader.'

Alice rolled her eyes.

Then it came to her. She held her breath and telepathised the words: 'Plan B'.

The band around the Mailboat device said, 'Please wait, processing…'

Then a status query appeared: 'Allow remote access?'

It was only a matter of seconds before Alice found herself consulting her watch, and entering the location of the chamber and the exact date and time for Karla's laptop to command the C-Bean to travel: 11/09/2118 12.35GMT.

It was only when Charlie suddenly leaped aside, wincing and hopping on one leg, that Alice realized the C-Bean had not only materialised but had almost crushed his foot.

The first to emerge from the C-Bean was Edie. Her face was pale and gaunt and she was shaking slightly. Behind her, Alice could see Hannah, rubbing her eyes and squinting.

'Edie, Hannah!' Alice said and rushed forwards to give them both a hug.

But they stood limply like ragdolls and said nothing.

'Where are the Sams? Where's Spex?' Charlie enquired. They still didn't speak.

'Hey, don't worry, it's really us, silly – and you're outside the lab, so you can talk now!' Alice assured them, and it suddenly came back to her that she had been too afraid to speak to Commander Hadron when she was being interrogated in the replica of her bedroom. Somehow he must have got her to speak eventually, because she could now remember roaring as loud as she could, over and over, 'LET ME OUT OF HERE PLEEEEEEASE!' She still couldn't remember what he had said to make her act that way, but she knew now it was the reason she had such a terrible sore throat when she woke up in the cleit…

Edie peered suspiciously through her glasses. She looked long and hard at Rudy before turning to examine Alice's face, as if she was looking for any anomalies that would confirm she was not who she appeared to be.

'It's really me, Edie, honest,' said Alice, and then added a piece of information that she thought would help convince her friend she was genuine: 'Spex was taken when I went to be interrogated. He's somewhere in the lab. We'll get him back too, don't worry.'

Edie still looked nervous and only half convinced. She hesitated for a moment, then rolled up her sleeve and wordlessly showed Alice the bioport on her arm.

'They did it to me too, Edie,' said Alice, patting the unit on her own arm. 'Here, let me untag you.' Alice pressed the button and held it down, counting under her breath. Edie winced with pain and tried to pull her arm away.

'I know it hurts, Edie, but once it's done they won't be able to detect where you are anymore.'

Edie's expression was more confused and frightened than ever.

'Rudy, can I have two more of the "sniff" things for my friends? They're going to need oxygen now, too.'

Finally it was Hannah who spoke.

'Who's Rudy?'

Rudy stepped forward with a big smile on his face, holding out two orange packages. Alice started to unwrap them and explain what they were to the girls, but they both looked terrified and ran back inside the C-Bean. Edie was shaking with fear.

'Edie's completely traumatised, isn't she?' Alice sighed.

'She must have gone through the same thing we did. I bet that's where the Sams are right now – that's why they're not in the C-Bean,' Charlie said as he inserted the Mark 3 cardkey into the slot in the C-Bean's access panel. Rudy was watching him intently, his yellow eyes bright with curiosity.

'That means they won't have interrogated Hannah yet, since she's the youngest,' Alice surmised.

'Or tagged her. I bet she doesn't have an oxygen port fitted. She'll have to use a cylinder.'

Charlie took another rebreather out of the crate beside the airlock door and they both stepped inside the C-Bean. Edie and Hannah were cowering in the corner. It smelt of unwashed bodies and stale air. But almost as soon as Alice noticed this, a newer, fresher smell swept through the pod. Without being prompted, the C-Bean produced several sets of clean clothes, all folded neatly in their own recess in the wall. A bowl of clean water appeared in a recess on the opposite wall, together with fluffy towels, a soap dispenser, a tube of toothpaste and five new toothbrushes. She realised the C-Bean must be back to its old cooperative self if this was happening.

'Time for a wash and brush up, guys! My teeth sure do feel furry,' said Charlie, peeling off his pyjama top.

'Who's the fifth one for?' Hannah asked in a raspy whisper.

Alice counted the faces in the pod. Then she stuck her head outside the door. Rudy was standing guard outside.

'Why are you out here, Rudy?'

'Keep Eye open,' he explained, 'Not want AFOS21XV find Blackbox.'

'Is that the namecode of the guard who was after you?'

Rudy nodded and pointed at the airlock door.

'He Cyborg. Can come back. Stop Blackbox.'

'Don't worry, Rudy. You'll be safe inside the C-Bean. I mean, the Blackbox seems to be working normally again now.'

Rudy stepped tentatively into the pod. Alice held her breath, waiting to see if her hunch was correct. Sure enough, the C-Bean didn't scan Rudy in that same unfriendly way it had scanned them upon arrival, and she decided it was therefore no longer under Hadron's command now that it was outside his compound.

As if to prove it was no longer their enemy, once the children had washed and changed into the clean clothes and were busy brushing their teeth, the C-Bean produced a huge picnic hamper, even bigger than the one Alice had left for the starving St Kildans back in 1851. Charlie and Rudy lifted the hamper down and Alice opened the lid to find that it was full of delicious food for them: perfectly ripe bananas, sticky buns, warm sausage rolls, little tangerines, cherry tomatoes, fat juicy grapes and chocolate biscuits. Alice picked up a biscuit and demolished it in one mouthful. It tasted just like the one she had imagined the first time she ever went inside the C-Bean.

Hannah crept out of the corner and stole a grape.

'Edie, it's real food!' she said, savouring it slowly.

Edie shot a look at Alice, then darted forward and grabbed a banana from the hamper. Rudy was watching her, utterly fascinated, as she peeled back the skin in strips and started eating.

'Would you like a banana too, Rudy?' Alice asked.

'What is Bana-na?'

'It's a fruit. It grows in bunches on a tree,' explained Alice, gesturing with her hand. 'Have you never seen one before?'

'No. Never see Banana. Never eat Fruit. No Fruit now. Grandpa show Picture. When Boy, he eat Fruit.'

In the end, the children devoured everything in sight and at the end of the meal the C-Bean produced a large jug of water and a set of paper cups.

'I want to go home,' Hannah announced tearfully when they had all finished. She started to cry.

'We can't go home just yet, Hannah, not until we figure out a way to get the Sams back. We can't go back to 2018 without them, can we?' Alice coaxed, stroking Hannah's hair.

Charlie had a very particular look on his face, like he'd just had an idea.

'Look, the Sams must be somewhere inside Hadron's lab right? So let's just open the airlock exit where Rudy escaped – maybe they'll figure it out and come running.'

'Problem. Rudy open Airlock. Buzz Buzz. AFOS21XV come.' Rudy put his hands over his ears to show them just how loud the alarm would sound.

'Well, I can't think how else we're going to rescue them,' said Charlie in a resigned tone.

'OK, let's give it a try,' Alice agreed. 'Edie, Hannah and I will stay inside while you boys go and open the airlock, but they'd better be quick or we'll all be caught.'

Alice stood blocking the entrance after the two boys stepped out, because she didn't want the girls to see Rudy use the dead finger. She watched as Charlie shone Sam's torch on the airlock while Rudy pressed its fingerprint against the keypad to be scanned. When she heard the airlock seal open, she braced herself for the alarm going off, but none of them could have imagined just how loud it would be. Charlie dropped the torch and slammed his fingers in his ears. Rudy just winced and they both ran back to the C-Bean. Alice could hear something else amidst the alarm, another sound. Something unmistakably familiar. A bark. Just as Alice was closing the C-Bean door, a wet black nose appeared out of the darkness and pushed his way through the gap, tail wagging.

'Spex!'

The dog rushed around the pod, licking everyone hello, including Rudy. Charlie shut the door and the sound of the alarm halved in volume. Hannah was cuddling Spex and laughing until Edie pointed to one side of his body where all his fur had been shaved off and there was a ragged row of stitches.

'What have they done to you, Spex, your poor little mutt?' Alice cried. 'Oh, I wish the Sams would hurry up, so we can get out of here.' She noticed Spex was making quite a fuss of Rudy. 'Have you met our dog before, Rudy?'

'Yes. Know Bork. Meet inside Lab. Sleep by Rudy Cell. Give him Food. Cry in Night. Scar hurting.'

'He's not really called Bork, you know.' Alice tickled the dog's tummy and saw that Spex was still wearing the black-and-gold disk that said 'Børk'. 'Someone else put that thing round his neck.'

She still hadn't worked out how or why Spex came back that day in Liverpool. Was it some kind of side-effect of resetting the C-Bean a day into the future – had they opened up a tiny glitch in time and he'd fallen through from 1960? Or had someone engineered an exchange remotely, taking their parrot Spix hostage in exchange for Spex? She remembered how faithfully Spex had stayed beside the injured Donald in 1944, keeping him company in that lonely valley until help came. It was nice to think that Rudy had done the same thing for the wounded Spex.

'Can't we just go home now?' Hannah pleaded, bringing Alice out of her reverie.

'Yes, TS100 now,' urged Rudy.

'I've got another idea: Rudy, pass me the Mailboat, quickly!'

Alice held the device and mentally entered what she assumed would be the two Sams' namecodes: SFIT2011 and SJAC2011. Their replies came almost in unison, a string of blue letters racing around the perimeter of the device: 'Alice, is that you? It says AROB2007. We're inside this weird round room with spongy blue spikes. Where are you?'

Alice thought quickly.

'Boys, you need to get out of there. The rest of us are all here in the C-Bean waiting for you. We've opened Airlock 01 – that's why the alarm's gone off – so you haven't got long before Hadron's people work out what's happened. We've brought the C-Bean up to the chamber beneath the gun, just the other side of the airlock exit. With any luck when you get here it'll be invisible. Come immediately!'

More blue letters from both of them, this time saying 'OK. Roger that!'

Alice put the Mailboat down and muttered the invisible command to the C-Bean, and they all waited.

And waited.

The alarm outside suddenly cut out.

Silence.

Out of the corner of her eye, Alice noticed another message scrolling around the Mailboat device. She was just about to pick it up and read what it said when the C-Bean broke the silence. The walls suddenly started pulsing with light, and a robotic voice said over and over:

INITIATING EMERGENCY INTERVENTION PROTOCOL.
COMMENCING REMOTE OVERRIDE AND RESTRICTED ACCESS.
PROCESS CANNOT BE INTERRUPTED.

Alice barked 'Manual override!' but the C-Bean did not respond.

Quick as a flash, Charlie grabbed Karla's laptop and tried to perform a remote override with her username. It allowed him system access, but the laptop screen displayed exactly the same status message as they were hearing over the C-Bean's audio channel:

REMOTE OVERRIDE COMPLETE. RESTRICTED ACCESS IN OPERATION.
ONLY PRE-PROGRAMMED DESTINATIONS AVAILABLE.
SELECT ONE OF THE FOLLOWING OPTIONS:
1)   TEST SITE 01: E.D.
2)   TEST SITE 02: Ø.F.
3)   TEST SITE 03: H.S.

The last option was greyed out – Alice then realised that H.S. must stand for Hadron Services – and was therefore greyed out because they were already at that location. A cursor blinked on and off, waiting for a command. None of the children spoke, afraid this was another trick. After a minute or so, a system prompt came up:

YOU HAVE 30 SECONDS REMAINING TO MAKE YOUR SELECTION.
FAILURE TO SELECT WILL RESULT IN PERMANENT SHUT DOWN OF THIS
C-BEAN MARK 4.

'OK, guys, we have to do something,' Charlie urged.

'Yes, but which one?'

'I vote we go for Test Site One, E.D. Get it? "Edie"! What could go wrong with that?' Charlie joked, rolling his eyes at Edie, but Alice knew that in reality he was feeling terrified.

She cleared her throat.

'Test Site 01. Now.'

The emergency intervention had obviously made the C-Bean Mark 4 very unstable. The system would run for a while, then, without any warning, crash and reboot. Alice couldn't tell whether they had actually departed for Test Site 01 or not. Meanwhile, the C-Bean kept trying to show them an information briefing, but it had stopped and started so many times that Alice wasn't sure if she had understood things correctly. From what she could make out, Test Site 01 seemed to be some sort of gold recovery and production centre, located somewhere in the Amazon Basin, judging by the glimpse of a map of Brazil they were shown.

On all four walls around them, the C-Bean now displayed various snippets of old video footage of gold being mined at this location in the 21st century. There had evidently been some kind of gold rush there. Alice saw clips of trees being felled, gold being panned and men in suits shaking hands about some deal that had been struck. It was when she saw footage of a bulldozer digging the claggy yellow earth to make a new building that Alice started to wonder if it was the same place where they'd found the gold nugget. A date flashed up quickly – 2025 – and the voiceover explained how the world changed from using paper money that year and went back to using gold as the main global currency. It appeared that countries without gold to mine seized all the gold belonging to their people instead – there were images of men and women standing in long queues, forced to hand over wedding rings, watches and jewellery – and then a bit of a documentary showing how all of this was melted down and turned into rectangular ingots or tokens that were the new money system. Alice saw piles of the tokens glinting in vaults, each one stamped with a number. Then the walls went blank again as the C-Bean's system went down for the fifth time.

'There's something spookily familiar about all this, Charlie. Do you think it's the same place we found the gold nugget in 2018?' Alice asked slowly.

'Yeah, maybe we were sent there on purpose back in January – maybe the gold nugget was put there for us to find.'

'And Spix too.' Edie spoke for the first time.

'But why?' Alice half whispered.

The C-Bean's system came back up again before anyone could reply. It was as if it was trying to answer her question – apparently shortages of real gold meant that people started to experiment with making gold out of other metals, mercury in particular, whose chemical structure was not that different from gold. They found that if they changed the mercury particles using a nuclear process, they could fabricate gold quite easily. But the problem was not only that this was a very expensive thing to do, but also that the resulting gold was radioactive. However, it was still circulated on the black market, which meant that many people got sick from handling it and died.

All Alice could think about were the globules of mercury spilled on the forest floor, the mercury they'd accidentally spilled into the sea when they'd crashed the C-Bean on the rocks coming back from Australia, and the nuclear leak they'd discovered in the hollowed-out chamber on St Kilda that had given their fathers radiation sickness…

The C-Bean continued with its little lecture. Since 2060, improvements had been made to the synthetic production of gold. Scientists came up with the idea of using a giant particle accelerator 100 km in diameter to produce a non-radioactive version. Then, in 2089, a group of 'TS50 engineers' who had been working for CERN in Switzerland in 2039 on the new Hadron Antimatter Collider, defected to Brazil to build the giant accelerator at a top-secret facility, El Dorado.

Upon hearing the words Hadron and El Dorado in the same sentence, Alice's jaw dropped open. Edie and Charlie were also gawping at each other, speechless.

'So that's what E.D. really stands for – El Dorado,' Charlie said finally in a low voice. 'And yes, Alice, in answer to your question we have been here before.'

None of it meant anything to Rudy, of course, who had no idea the others had come here by accident one day back in January. While Charlie, Edie and Alice were still trying to figure out why they might have been brought here again, Rudy was busy staring at the walls because they looked like they were about to disintegrate.

'But what do they mean by "TS50 engineers", Charlie? Didn't Rudy say something about TS100? Rudy?' Alice's voice trailed away as she realised that Spex had scampered off through the porous remains of the C-Bean's walls into the space beyond, with Rudy following.

Alice and Charlie looked at each other. Edie grabbed Hannah's hand and started to walk off after them.

'Get the cardkey, Charlie – let's go.'

The part of the rainforest they'd arrived in looked dull, dusty and a lot less dense than Alice remembered. The overall impression was of masses of tall grey tree trunks against a gloomy grey sky. Up ahead were a high perimeter fence and a set of security gates with that familiar green-and-yellow El Dorado logo fixed to them, beside a post bristling with surveillance cameras. It was eerily quiet. Alice remembered the roar of insects and animals, the lush vegetation and the din of a waterfall the last time the C-Bean brought them here. This time there was no greenery – in fact no sign of any wildlife at all. Nor could she hear the waterfall. She ran to catch up with Rudy and Spex.

Rudy turned and pointed to a metal grille in the base of one of the trees, just where its roots spread into the ground. He put his finger to his lips for them to keep quiet. Alice noticed that all the trees had something similar, and from one or two of the grilles she saw a puff of steamy air emerging. Rudy seemed to be leading them away from the gates and into a part of the forest where there was a gap in the trees. He stopped and turned to face Alice with a distraught look on his face.

'What's the matter, Rudy?' Alice whispered.

'Is not good. All Trees here 3DPOs.'

'What does that mean?'

'I think he's saying they're fake,' Edie said bluntly. 'Some of them back there had loudspeakers in them.' She tapped one of the trunks and, sure enough, there was a resounding hollow sound. Rudy nodded vigorously. Alice bent down to examine a leaf that appeared to have fallen from one of the trees. It looked real enough but, when she handled it, it crumbled away into a fine green dust in her hand.

'They print Trees. Make look real 3D. No real Forest left now. Make animals too. Not like Bork. He real Dog.'

They walked a bit further. It was ferociously hot.

'So, no insects either? Is that why it's so quiet?'

'Tried print Bees. Not work. That why no Fruit,' Rudy explained, shaking his head.

Alice looked down at her feet. The ground felt real enough – it was still the same claggy yellow soil she remembered from last time. And the gold nugget must have been real, too, if Lori got so much money for it in Glasgow. But Alice now realised it was not something that had been dug out of the ground. For all she knew, it was a man-made lump of radioactive gold.

'Look out!'

A green-and-yellow flatbed truck came into view carrying wooden crates of some kind. They all ducked behind a tree as it sped past. Spex had picked up an invisible scent trail and seemed to know where he was going. He ran after the truck, and the children followed him. Ahead there were several discarded broken crates lying on the ground. Spex started sniffing the crates and wagging his tail. Alice gasped when she got close enough to read the label on one of them. It said:

LIVE SPECIES COURTESY OPERATION SEABEAN DELIVERY DATE: 13 JUNE 2114

Charlie pointed for them to follow the truck, which was heading slowly towards a building just inside the security gates. As the gates started to slide open, Rudy leapt forwards, grabbed hold of the handle on the tailgate and jumped on the back of the truck, beckoning to the others to do the same. Edie and Hannah hung back but Alice and Charlie managed to leap up. Alice could see the back of the driver's head in the cab, wearing a green-and-yellow baseball cap. The dog trotted along behind the truck and, just before the gates slid shut, he ducked inside too, leaving Edie and Hannah watching forlornly from outside the El Dorado compound. Alice signalled for them to stay there, and Edie nodded gravely.

The truck drove into the delivery bay of the first building. Inside it was much cooler and quite dark. Alice could see row upon row of storage racking, ten metres high or more, and decided it was a vast warehouse. Spex suddenly darted off to the left down one of the aisles of racking marked 'M' and stopped to investigate one particular crate that had been deposited there. Rudy jumped down and followed him and, by the time Charlie and Alice did the same, the dog had ripped the whole side off. Suddenly a flurry of green, blue and yellow feathers surged into the air, almost in slow motion, the colours appearing to change from blue to green and back again. A label on the piece of crate by Alice's feet said 'Macaw Clones, derived from 2014 sample type SP045'. Once they started squawking, Alice realised they were all parrots. Then all at once from amongst the squawking came a lone cry, like a small, lost child:

'*Muito mau, perigroso!*'

Alice rapidly scanned the seething mass of parrots – could it be? Or was she just imagining things? But who should rise up into the air and descend onto Alice's shoulder but an old friend, bobbing his head and tugging a strand of her hair with his beak.

'Spix! However did you get here?' Alice whispered incredulously. The bird moved from side to side along her shoulder, swaying to and fro as if he couldn't quite account for his whereabouts either. Spex started barking excitedly and jumping up to say hello to the parrot.

There were voices coming from the warehouse entrance and a torch beam suddenly flashed into the aisle. Alice glanced behind her and could see the silhouette of the truck driver walking towards them, scanning the aisle with his torch. Rudy quickly pulled Charlie and Alice behind the crate and they hid in the shadows. Charlie held Spex's muzzle to stop him from barking. Through the gaps in the crate they could see the parrots flapping around the truck driver, who was batting them away with his arms as he struggled to get something out of his pocket. He muttered something and then there was a single phut! like a shot from a gun with a silencer. All the parrots immediately stopped making a noise and dropped to the ground simultaneously, apart from Spix. Alice stared in horror at the carpet of blue-and-green birds, unable to fathom how the man had killed all of them with one shot. The truck driver grunted, then cleared a path between the creatures with his feet and walked off.

When he'd gone, Charlie picked up one of the inert parrots. There was no sign of any blood or injury and his eyes were still open.

'Is it dead?' Alice breathed, stroking the feathers.

'I don't think so, it's like he's been… switched off,' replied Charlie with a puzzled look on his face.

'They not real Bird. They cyborg too,' Rudy remarked, turning the creature over and showing them a panel under its tail bearing a printed 'UAT' serial number and the words 'CHICO® Colour-Changing Artificial Macaw. Made in Brazil'. Rudy then flicked a tiny switch on the side of the bird's beak and it began to ruffle its feathers and come alive again. It flew out of Charlie's hands and over to join Spix, who had perched on the edge of the storage racking.

'Olá!' Spix said cheerily to his cloned double, checking him out.

'Ooaa!' replied his cybernetic friend.

'Hmmm. Looks like there's room for improvement with Chico's mimic function,' joked Charlie.

Just then, a deafening announcement in Portuguese came over the audio system:

'AVISO: GUARDA PROTEÇÂO A CORREDOR "M". INTRUSO!'

'Come on – I think that means we need to get out of here,' Charlie hissed.

They ran to the end of the aisle and back into the delivery bay where the truck was parked. A security guard had just arrived with an enormous wolf-like creature straining on a leash. Spex slunk behind Alice, sensing he was no match for it. Rudy jumped up inside the cab of the truck and pressed a button that made the security gates start to open.

'Run!' Rudy shouted to Charlie and Alice, pointing to the gates.

Then he turned, strode towards the security guard, grabbed the wolf's collar with one hand, and then swung his other arm back in one fluid motion, landing a massive punch on the security guard's chin. Alice ran past just as the man's limbs crumpled under him and he fell to the ground. She watched Rudy feel inside one of the wolf's ears to find the switch and immobilise the cybernetic animal.

'Vamos, vamos!' fretted Spix, hovering nervously over the entire scene. Alice started running again.

Edie and Hannah appeared from behind some fake bushes opposite the gates and they all sprinted as fast as they could between the fake trees, back towards the spot where they'd arrived. Sweat was dripping into Alice's eyes. She wiped her face on her sleeve and looked up ahead. She could see Spex bounding along beside Rudy, Edie and Hannah clinging to each other as they ran, Spix whirling around in circles over their heads, and Charlie out in front staring hard at the C-Bean's cardkey, willing the globe to spin and show him the way. Would their Mark 3 key still work? The C-Bean somehow didn't seem to be in a stable state. But that was nothing compared to the state of the world in 2118, where it appeared everything was, well... ruined. She had never felt so homesick in her whole life – she desperately wanted to get back home to St Kilda in 2018, back to where there was a real tree, real birds and real air, where the sky wasn't a crazy colour and where the village wasn't half under water – and, most of all, to where her family was all still in one piece.

The C-Bean Mark 4 presented them with only one pre-programmed option this time – they had no choice but to select 'Test Site 03: H.S.' and return to St Kilda, 2118.

'What if we arrive back inside the lab?' asked Edie. 'I can't bear the thought of going back inside there.'

Alice tried to input the coordinates she remembered for their schoolyard and even tried to request a different date, but the C-Bean responded with a pre-recorded announcement, similar to the one they'd heard when they were first abducted:

ANY ACTS INVOLVING MALICIOUS DAMAGE TO THE NATURAL COURSE
OF EVENTS AND WILFUL MANIPULATION OF STATUTORY TIME ARE
STRICTLY FORBIDDEN AND UNDER PRESENT LAW IF CONVICTED CARRY
THE HARSHEST PENALTY: TS100.

'What on earth does that mean?' Charlie asked of no one in particular.
'It mean bad News.' Rudy looked glum.

'Rudy, can you please explain all this TS business? I don't understand,' Alice said impatiently.

'TS mean timeshift. People come from Before. Like You. You TS100 – I see Namecode 2018. Jump 100 Year. Most TS50. Bring for Knowhow.'

'Like those TS50 engineers, you mean? The ones they recruited from CERN to work on the El Dorado project?'

Rudy nodded.

'So does this TS100 penalty mean that the punishment for messing around with time is to send you another 100 years into the future – like to 2218?'

Another nod.

Judging by the terrible state of things in 2118, Alice couldn't begin to imagine what kind of worse fate awaited the poor person who received that kind of punishment.

'Is time travel illegal?' Edie enquired hopefully.

'Not allowed go Backwards, only Forwards. But still do. Black Market. People want go back whole Century, minus 100. Want swap for better Life. Want real Food. Want free Sniff. Want no War. Make People from Before come here. Swap. Timeshift in Blackbox. Costs much Gold.'

Alice allowed this new information to sink in, and it triggered a whole new set of questions in her head: Who had brought them to 2118, and why? Was it because someone wanted their knowhow? But what could a bunch of schoolkids know? Or had there been some case of mistaken identity? Was that why Dr Foster appeared in Liverpool, to warn her they were about to be abducted – is that why he said there was something wrong with the C-Bean? Or had they been kidnapped by Hadron Services in order that some people from 2118 could swap places with them? Were they simply here because someone had paid a fortune for the privilege of being taken back to 2018, to take their places and be able to live a better life? Did that mean Alice and her classmates were the unwitting victims of this illegal black-market time-travel operation? And, if so, were they now stranded in 2118 for ever? Rudy was their only way to get answers.

'Is that what Hadron Services do, Rudy? Help people timeshift?'

'Yes. Fix Blackbox for Timeshift.'

'Have you ever met Commander Hadron, Rudy?'

'He bad Man. Many Enemy. This his Finger,' Rudy informed her proudly, patting his pocket.

Alice grimaced and decided she would rather not know how he had come by Commander Hadron's index finger. The very thought of it made her feel sick. Without realising it, she had been pacing around the C-Bean with Spex and Spix following her, while Charlie, Rudy, Edie and Hannah lay in the middle on a pile of sleeping bags.

'What does he want with us?' she murmured. 'It doesn't make any sense.'

There was an abrupt judder, and the C-Bean seemed to bounce slightly. Alice felt a sharp pain in her lower stomach. She clutched her belly and saw that the others were doing the same. The C-Bean went into another shutdown cycle and then started to reboot. Lines of computer code scrolled up the walls and then they heard a further announcement:

WELCOME TO 2118. MY NAME IS COMMANDER HADRON. AS EXCLUSIVE AND VALUED MEMBERS OF OUR REVOLUTIONARY TS100 PROGRAMME, YOU WILL NOW UNDERGO A COMPREHENSIVE INDUCTION SESSION WITH ONE OF HADRON SERVICES' AGENTS. YOU HAVE BEEN ASSIGNED AGENT AFOS21XV.

Hearing this made Rudy's yellow eyes go wide with fear and he scrambled to his feet. It was the same namecode of the guard who had pursued him when he'd escaped.

'Rudy take Agent,' he said, asserting himself. Everyone was startled by Rudy's sudden change of mood. Alice watched as he increased the flow rate on his oxygen unit, flipped open the silver penknife, rolled back his shoulders and then stood in front of the exit door, poised and ready to spring into action as soon as it opened.

A voice queried: 'Passenger verification' and the C-Bean responded by supplying an alphabetical arrival list of its five passengers:

AROB2007

CCHE2006

EBUR2007

HBUR2010

RBOK2104

The voice confirmed this information – 'Verification complete' – and the door to the C-Bean opened.

Standing outside the meet them was a man with white curly hair, wearing sneakers and a grey duffle coat. It was none other than Dr Foster. He smiled at the children and stepped forward.

'Welcome. I am your agent, AFOS21XV, but you can call me Dr Foster. I hope you had a pleasant journey,' he said in a flat monotone. 'Rudy, may I have my knife back, please?'

In one move, Rudy leapt towards him and rugby-tackled him to the ground. He seemed to be struggling to take something off Dr Foster's wrist. Alice could see that her teacher was still wearing some kind of identity bracelet. Dr Foster's limbs were flailing around uselessly.

'Charlie, help! Need neutralise Cyborg.'

'Don't worry Rudy, that man's not a cyborg – he's our old teacher, Dr Foster,' Hannah assured him, looking relieved to see a familiar face at last. Spex was not so sure, and started barking.

Alice tried to step forward to stop Rudy from hurting Dr Foster, but Spix started making a fuss.

'*Muito mau, muito mau!*' the parrot warned, strangely agitated by the sight of the agent.

'Hannah, Alice, stay back! Rudy might be right – maybe he's fake too,' Edie said, looking horrified at the three bodies grappling in front of them.

Dr Foster's face seemed to be going through a whole collection of different expressions, as if rehearsing a palette of emoticons. When Charlie finally managed to remove the bracelet, Alice watched in astonishment as Dr Foster's head twitched a little and then rotated a full 360 degrees before coming back to its original position with the eyes shut.

'Safe now,' panted Rudy. 'Quick, we go.'

Alice had been so shocked by the bizarre reappearance of Dr Foster and the realisation that he was clearly not who she thought, that she hadn't even noticed where they had arrived. But, judging by the look on Edie's face, it was exactly as she'd feared – they were in one of Hadron's laboratories. Surrounding the C-Bean were trolleys with stainless steel instruments laid out, and on a desk in the corner Alice saw a laptop just like Karla's that had been partially dismantled. Alice walked across the room to take a closer look.

'C'mon Alice, we haven't got time to look around,' urged Charlie. 'I've got the cardkey – now let's just go!'

Alice turned to look at the C-Bean. She was worried that if they left it here in the lab with these instruments, the people in the green gowns with masks might take their C-Bean apart too – like they did to Spex, judging by his scars – and then they would never be able to get back to 2018.

She suddenly felt exhausted and overwhelmed by everything that had happened. The C-Bean was their only link to home in this cruel future world. A small tear welled up in the corner of her eye but, just as it began to roll down her cheek, the C-Bean wobbled in sympathy and obediently disappeared. Alice let out a sigh of relief.

'Alice, come!' Rudy had opened the pale green door with the circular vision panel and was leading everyone out and back into the long curving corridor. It was icy cold compared to the fake forest in Brazil, and her breath was forming in a cloud in front of her face. Spix suddenly landed on her shoulder and gripped tight. Rudy was heading for the airlock, the others running along behind him in single file and Spex weaving in between their legs. When they reached the airlock, Rudy touched the control pad with the severed finger and quickly ushered the children through, just as the deafening alarm flared up.

Rudy slammed the airlock door shut and the alarm stopped. They all stood panting in the dark chamber beneath the gun emplacement, ears ringing and hearts pumping, reeling from the events of the past ten minutes. It was only after they'd got their breath back, and Charlie found he had Sam's wind-up torch in his pocket, that they realised the hatch at the top of the ladder was securely closed up.

'We're trapped!' cried Alice in dismay, feeling just like she imagined Karla did when she was claustrophobic.

'Great! So let me get this right – we manage to get away from the fake jungle, out of the C-Bean, away from that weirdo version of Dr Foster, then escape from Hadron's lab, only to find we're on St Kilda but it's still 2118 and we're in a worse mess than ever,' groaned Edie.

Hannah started to cry. 'Poor Dr Foster,' she sobbed. Spex went up to her and licked her hand in sympathy.

Rudy climbed up the ladder to inspect the underside of the hatch, but there was obviously no way of rotating the gun to open it from the inside. He pummelled it angrily with his fists and grumbled some words in a language that Alice didn't understand. The wind-up torch clicked off and they were plunged into darkness again. She heard Rudy climb back down the ladder and rummage in his bag for something. Alice could see the blue light of the Mailboat device receiving a message. Rudy frowned and looked like he was about to reply, but suddenly changed his mind and hurled it against the roof of the chamber in a frustrated outburst.

The Mailboat clanged off the rock and landed somewhere near Edie's feet. She knelt down to look for it.

'Hey, steady on, mate. No need to lose the plot just yet,' said Charlie reproachfully.

'Is more Trouble now – we all get TS100,' Rudy snorted and kicked a loose rock but said nothing about what he had just learned. Alice realised the message he'd received must have been to inform him that they all faced the punishment of being shipped to 2218.

'Charlie, can I have the torch please?' Alice asked quietly.

Charlie wound it up again and flashed it on, pointing it to where she was kneeling. The Mailboat lay in pieces on the ground next to their time capsule.

'It's broken, isn't it?' sobbed Hannah.

'Now what do we do?' Edie shrieked, glaring at Rudy, who stared helplessly back at her. 'Rudy, that was really stupid. For a start you could have really hurt someone. And now we don't have any means of communicating with anyone outside this cave!' she added petulantly.

Edie's tone of voice reminded Alice of the time her sister Lori was having a go at her and, in that same moment, Alice realised she was so homesick she was even missing Lori. She bent down to gather up the broken pieces and, as she opened the lid of the time capsule to clear the broken Mailboat away, her hand brushed past something that hadn't been there before. The torch switched off.

'Charlie, the torch – quick, wind it up again!' she said in an urgent whisper.

'What is it?'

'Someone's left a note inside the time capsule.'

Alice's Blog #4

Wednesday 12th September 2018

Just as I was reading out the note from Sam F saying they had escaped and were going to hide out in the old schoolroom and wait for us, we heard voices above ground. There was a lot of grinding and scraping as someone tried to get the hatch open. We didn't realise then, but it was the Sams. They'd found a metal pole and bit by bit managed to get the rusty hatch to budge. Suddenly they flipped it open, Spix flew up into the sky and we all climbed out. They were a bit surprised to see this tall black kid with us, but Rudy had calmed down by then and even managed a friendly grin.

As it was raining hard when we got above ground, we ran round to the chapel to take cover. The Sams told us breathlessly how they were chased by 'some guy who looked just like Dr Foster' but that he tripped over and they got away and hid in a cleit. We told them he was there to meet us when we arrived back in the C-Bean and when Rudy added 'He Cyborg. He Hadron guard' the two Sams gawped at each other going 'No way! To be honest, the rest of us are still trying to get our heads around the fact that our teacher was an imposter.

Then, just as Rudy was about to untag the boys' bioports and get them sorted with oxygen units, who should walk into the chapel but

Reverend Sinclair! 'Ah, children, thank God, you've come back! We have all been praying so hard for your safe return. Hallelujah!' The vicar was so overjoyed to see us again he didn't even notice Rudy. Instead he ran out of the chapel, proclaiming 'a miracle has befallen the good people of St Kilda'.

We all just stood there in a daze. Rudy asked in a quiet voice, 'We timeshift? TS100? This your Time?' I went over to the window to check. I could just about make out through the dreary rain that the tide was out, our white sandy beach was right where it should be, and both the sea and the sky seemed to be back to normal. No flooding in the Bay, no weird colours in the sky, just some nice plain old Scottish rain. I had never felt so happy in my entire life! I ran outside and the others followed and we all pranced round the schoolyard, seven children, a dog and the parrot all doing a silly little dance, singing songs and getting soaking wet. But we didn't care.

I still haven't worked out what happened yesterday – it was as if the C-Bean's powers had seeped out into that underground chamber and let us time travel back to 2018 without the pod itself actually being there, just like when I found myself back in the present with Lady Grange. Perhaps it was because Charlie still had the Mark 3 cardkey in his pocket. When he gave it back to me, the black cube loomed into view in the middle of where we were dancing. The door opened as if to say 'hi' and Rudy walked inside. He was laughing and crying at the same time. He stood in the middle of the pod and said triumphantly, 'I Timeshift! Rudy now City of Smiles. First time since little Boy.' Hearing him say that, the C-Bean produced a steaming bowl of rice and some chopsticks, and then started displaying pictures of Jutland on all its walls, like it was trying to make him feel really at home. Rudy grinned from ear to ear, ate the rice and chatted to us about the places he recognised. Then he curled up on the floor inside the pod like a baby and fell asleep with Spex by his side.

We left the two of them there to rest and walked off up Main Street, six tired, wet, happy children. Our parents came running out of our houses to meet us, and a lot more tears were shed.

When I tried to tell Mum and Dad everything that had happened since we went to sleep inside the C-Bean the night of our sleepover, at first they were really angry that we'd gone against their instructions. But I kept telling them we didn't do it on purpose – we were abducted – the C-Bean just got taken to 2118. Of course, it all sounded pretty crazy, so in the end they decided I was imagining things and needed to rest. It was when I started telling them about Commander Hadron's secret underground lab in 2118, and about Dr Foster being a cyborg, and about how we went to El Dorado with its fake trees, and that there are no birds or animals or fruit or bees in 2118, they just said 'Poor Alice, whatever's the matter with you?' The only thing Dad took any notice of was when I said 'You know, Dad, in the future everywhere is flooded. Even St Kilda. The sea was right up to Main Street. I saw it with my own eyes.' He looked at me, and said in a solemn voice, 'I'm sure you're right, Alice. The marine biologists who are coming over on Sunday just sent me an email with the latest report saying sea rise is unstoppable - our glaciers and ice caps will have melted away completely by then'.

Thursday 13th September 2018

Something awful happened this morning. While I was still in bed asleep, some people arrived in a helicopter to confiscate the C-Bean like they said they would, which is bad enough, but of course it means they also took it with stowaways inside – Rudy and Spex! When Mum and Mr McLintock went down to school at nine o'clock to sign for it to be taken away, they didn't think to check inside, and so the two pilots just attached the C-Bean to the helicopter and flew off.

Now my parents think I really have gone mad because when they told me the news at lunchtime I kept saying 'But what about Rudy and Spex? They were inside the C-Bean!' Mum sat by my bed and stroked my hair for ages saying there was nothing to worry about, I was home safe and sound. Poor Rudy, I hope he's OK. He's only just arrived in 2018, and now this happens. And Spex – he's been through more than enough already.

Friday 14th September 2018

It gets worse! Mum just got a phone call from the Ministry of Defence at eight o'clock this morning to say someone would be arriving on St Kilda shortly to impound the C-Bean so they could carry out a full investigation into the 'suspicious circumstances' that have been brought to their attention. Mum sounded all confused on the phone. She was trying to explain to the person on the other end that the C-Bean had already been taken away. I could tell by her tone of voice she was starting to think something didn't quite add up. Right now Mum and Dad are talking in the kitchen trying to figure out what could have happened. They're even mentioning some of the things I've been telling them about Rudy and stuff. Mum is really panicking. She said something about checking the paperwork, so Dad's gone back down to school to fetch all the forms Mum signed to have a closer look at them.

    PS You'll never believe it, but five minutes ago, Dad burst through the back door yelling 'Jen, did you realise the person who authorized the C-Bean's removal yesterday was Karla Ingermann?'

It was Saturday evening and Alice was at home looking after her baby brother Kit while her parents were round at the Burneys. She was having difficulty coming to terms with the fact that the C-Bean, Spex and Rudy were, more than likely, gone for good. Neither of her parents had been able to get any information about Karla Ingermann, and the two Ministry of Defence officers, who had arrived the previous day to fetch the C-Bean and were obliged to leave empty-handed, accused the people of St Kilda of withholding information and obstructing their investigation. Alice had tried her best to explain to the officers and to her parents what had really happened, but it just seemed to make matters worse.

Alice was expecting Charlie and Edie to arrive at any minute – they were going to watch a DVD together. There was a loud knock on the door. She thought Charlie was messing about, because usually he just walked straight in without knocking – no one ever locked their front door on St Kilda.

'Come in,' Alice yelled, tucking Kit into his cot.

There was a second knock, more urgent this time.

'What are you playing at, Charlie?' Alice frowned and went to the door.

There on her doorstep stood Rudy and a smaller, skinnier person dressed in black jeans with a black hoodie pulled over their face. Whoever it was also had their arms behind their back and Rudy appeared to have a firm grip on them. He pushed the person forwards and the hood fell down, revealing spiky red hair and a pale freckly face.

'Karla!' Alice gasped. She felt a strange frozen wrench in the pit of her stomach.

No one spoke. Alice could hear Kit murmuring in his cot. Her heart was beating fast. Karla was looking at the floor, a muscle twitching in her jaw. Rudy let out a loud sigh and Alice couldn't tell if he was exhausted or just exasperated.

'Rudy, are you OK? I'm so glad to see you! Whatever happened?'

'KROB2090 tell whole Story, Alice,' Rudy assured her, handing Alice the Mark 3 cardkey before leading Karla to the sofa, where he made her sit down.

'I should hope so. There are lots of things I'd like to know. Charlie and Edie will be here any second. You can tell all of us together,' Alice said firmly. The whole situation felt peculiarly formal. Alice realised this would be her chance to conduct her own interrogation. There was an awkward pause.

'Rudy, can I get you anything to eat or drink?'

Rudy shook his head and continued to stand guard behind the sofa in case Karla tried to escape. Finally, Alice heard the door open and Charlie and Edie walked into the living room carrying a bowl of home-made popcorn.

'We did it salty this time, Alice, 'cos we know you prefer it... Oh,' Edie's voice trailed away when she caught sight of the two extra people. Charlie raised his eyebrows.

'You didn't tell us it was going to be a party, Alice. We'd have brought more to eat,' he said wryly.

'I didn't know they were coming,' remarked Alice, wondering how this whole scene was going to play out. 'But apparently Karla can explain everything. So why don't you sit down?'

Karla sneezed loudly and asked for a tissue.

'I'm very allergic,' she said, a little too pitifully.

'Yes, we've noticed. You're always sniffing and sneezing. Why is that?' asked Alice, relieved to find an easy way to start the conversation.

'In 2118, where I come from, there is no real pollen. Every plant and every crop is pollinated artificially. There are no bees or butterflies.' She paused and Alice noticed something creep out from behind the sofa – it was Spex. Karla looked at the dog and rolled her eyes.

'I am also allergic to animal fur,' she continued. 'Where I come from, there are no real animals, either. So my body is not used to dealing with such things.'

'I see,' said Alice, patting Spex, who had lain down beside her. She was thrilled to have him back, but she couldn't afford to show it now, not while she was conducting this interrogation. What Karla was saying seemed to make sense in terms of what Rudy had told her.

'I take it that KROB2090 is your namecode and 2090 is your birthdate,' said Alice, doing a quick sum in her head. 'So you're 28, right?'

Karla nodded.

'But we know for a fact that Karla Ingermann is not your real name. Charlie found your passport. Everyone around here thinks you're an industrial spy working for a rival German company that's trying to steal the C-Bean idea from the people who really invented it. But I did begin to wonder if you were from the future. The label on your laptop says it was last checked on 1 April 2118, for a start. So who in actual fact are you, where do you come from and why did the C-Bean record your laptop as belonging to Karla Robertson?'

'Because my name *is* Karla Robertson.'

'Let's not play games, Karla. We need to know the truth now,' Alice said, trying not to get cross.

'I am telling the truth, Alice. Ingermann is the name of the suburb where I grew up. But my real name is Robertson. I work for Hadron Services. Commander Hadron owns all the rights to the C-Bean invention now – he inherited them from his old boss. I was originally sent here from 2118 to secure the safe return of Hadron Services' property – the C-Bean Mark 3. I didn't want to go, but Hadron insisted. After the C-Bean broke and the cyborg-supported mission went wrong, he said sending me was the only solution to get things back on track.'

'I don't get it. What mission?' Charlie demanded, glowering at Karla from the other side of the room.

'They realised that sending the cyborg Dr Foster to 2018 wasn't working when they started getting data reports from the C-Bean saying that the cyborg had lost control of the mission, so Hadron pulled him off the job. Then, to make matters worse, before he could send a replacement, you went off to Hong Kong and Australia unsupervised. They sent another cyborg to St Kilda, Melbourne, to try and steer you back on course. Remember the kumalak fortune-teller? That was also a cyborg, Alice ... '

'Who are you talking about?' interrupted Charlie.

'I think she means the fake Dr Foster, stupid,' Edie mumbled.

'So wait – let me get this straight. You're telling us that you work for Hadron's company in 2118 and they sent a C-Bean to St Kilda with a cyborg teacher in tow and then, when it didn't go according to plan, they sent you back in time instead to sort things out. But why?' Charlie was pacing up and down impatiently.

'Keep your voice down, Charlie. We don't want to wake Kit,' Alice whispered.

'Shut up, Alice. Who cares about your brother when we've got all this going on?' growled Charlie. 'So come on, Karla, answer me – why?'

'Because of the close match between our DNA,' Karla said quietly, biting her lip. She turned to face Alice. 'Look, I shouldn't be telling you this. But since everything's gone wrong, I might as well.'

'Tell me what?'

'Your brother is part of all this, Alice.'

'What do you mean?'

'Your brother – Kit Robertson – is my Dad.'

A whole new and unidentified feeling of rage and confusion surged through Alice's body. She stared at Karla unblinkingly.

'That's not possible,' she stuttered, once again doing the mental maths. 'My brother would be a hundred years old in 2118.'

'He timeshifted, Alice,' Karla's voice was softer and more gentle all of a sudden. 'You need to understand that after your dad was called up and then disappeared during World War III, and your mum got sick and died in 2029, your sister Lori had to look after Kit. It was not an easy time for either of them. The minute he left college he agreed to become a TS50 and moved to the future to work on a top-secret project at El Dorado in Brazil.'

Alice's brain was reeling with all this information concerning her family. It felt as if her head was full of those teeming particles, like the outer surface of the replica C-Bean she'd been taken to during her interrogation. She tried to keep her mind on the current situation, but bits and pieces kept flying out. She had this constant edgy feeling that there was no longer any overall stable pattern of events. Nothing could be thought of as having a strict chronological order, and everything seemed to loop round and join up to something else – Dr Foster,

Karla, her brother, El Dorado, Hadron. What next?

'So what you're saying is that Kit timeshifted fifty years, met someone…
and then you were born in 2090?' Alice asked slowly.

'I know this is awkward for you, Alice. You weren't meant to find out
like this. But you didn't cooperate with us during your interrogation like we
expected. They must have got your dosage or the psychological profiling
wrong. You wouldn't respond. Neither would Charlie. It's a shame because
Dad went to such a lot of trouble making your room. When it didn't work, he
had no choice but to put both you and Charlie in solitary de-confinement.
Except that you escaped. Just like the last time, when you abandoned me in
1918. I was so frightened there. I thought I'd never get home again. It was
your fault I got stuck there as a prisoner of war, Alice. But you – it's like you
and the C-Bean are one seamless entity, and you can just control it with the
power of your own thought! Dad told me everything would be fine, that it
would be an easy first job. But it was a lie and I'm still angry. When I finally
escaped from Donald's time back to 2118, Dad just said he had no idea you
would have so much control over the C-Bean. It took me forever to figure out
a way to make the C-Bean come back and fetch me. I don't understand why
I have so little influence over it – I passed all the training with top marks!'
Karla protested tearfully, the muscles in her jaw tensing up again.

'Hang on a minute!' Alice said, raising her arms as if to protect herself
from this latest onslaught. 'Forget Donald and all that 1918 nonsense for a
moment. So are you seriously trying to tell me that your Dad – my brother –
is Commander Hadron?'

Karla didn't reply. She wouldn't look Alice in the eye. Her breathing
sounded strange. She sniffed and then her head flopped forward, the hood
falling over her face.

'Karla, speak to me!'

After Karla collapsed and they couldn't seem to rouse her, Charlie and Rudy
carried her into Alice's bedroom and laid her on the bed.

'She funny Colour,' Rudy observed.

'But she is still breathing, right?' Edie asked, taking off Karla's hoodie and grabbing her wrist to feel her pulse, like she'd seen her mum do on countless occasions. 'Charlie, get her a glass of water, will you?'

'What are we going to do with her? And Rudy? Where are they going to stay?' Edie was fretting when Charlie returned with the drink.

'Who cares?' said Charlie. 'It's not our problem.'

'Well, in my opinion, it is our problem,' Edie insisted. 'I mean, if it wasn't for us taking off in the C-Bean in the first place, we wouldn't be in this situation. Alice, what do you think?' Edie turned round and realised that Alice had not left the living room. 'Charlie, go and see if Alice is alright. She must be feeling pretty shaken up by everything Karla let out just then.'

Charlie found Alice beside Kit's cot, stroking his downy red hair. There were tears rolling down her face.

'You know, he does kind of look like Karla, when you think about it. They have the same colour hair, and his nose is a bit similar, too,' she said miserably.

'Look, I know this is about as weird as it gets – meeting your brother's kid from the future and finding out about all the crappy things that lie ahead for your parents and everything – but we can't wind back time now to where we didn't know all of this stuff, Alice. So we're just going to have to deal with it, figure it all out, and maybe try to use what we know to make things less bad than they might otherwise be.'

'How do you mean?'

'Well, like we used time travel to make our dads better, get rid of that nuclear dump, save those babies from dying, and rescue Donald so he didn't die, remember? We've already moved mountains, Alice! Think what else we could do with this kind of knowledge about the future.'

Alice shrugged and dried her eyes.

'You're right. I just can't think about it right now. Maybe tomorrow.'

'OK. Hey, I've had an idea – how about Karla stays with Lady Grange this evening?'

'Mmm.'

'She won't ask any questions. We could ask Rudy to keep watch – sleep on the sofa or something – to make sure Karla doesn't run off or do anything stupid.'

'Whatever you think is best,' said Alice absent-mindedly.

Between them, Charlie and Rudy managed to escort Karla back down Main Street to Lady Grange's cottage. The cool autumn breeze seemed to revive her when they went outside and, by the time they knocked on Lady Grange's front door, Karla was able to walk by herself. Lady Grange appeared in a nightgown holding her ornate candlestick. She stared at them with a puzzled expression and seemed a little bit tipsy.

'What is it, Charlie my dear?' she hiccupped.

'Do you have room for two visitors, Lady Grange? They just arrived today. Like you did, erm … from another time. It's all a bit hush-hush, you know. The other grown-ups don't know yet. They just need somewhere to sleep.'

Lady Grange held the candle up to have a better look at Karla.

'You look familiar,' she slurred. 'I've seen those clothes before. Do I know you?'

Karla didn't speak.

'She's Alice's niece, Lady Grange.'

'I see.'

'The other visitor is a poor boy from Jutland who hasn't seen his family for years, like you,' Charlie said, artfully appealing to Lady Grange's sympathies.

At first Lady Grange looked doubtfully at Rudy, who responded with a quick flash of his toothless grin. She pursed her lips for a moment, and then handed Rudy the candlestick.

'You poor child. Ah, how I long to see my lovely babies. So far, far away. Come inside, dear boy. You look famished. I have some nice leftover stew you can eat.'

Alice's Blog #5

Sunday 16th September 2018, 11am

I hardly know where to start. A lot has happened since Rudy kidnapped Karla and brought her back to St Kilda in the C-Bean. It was very brave of him – but then I'm sure he must have been so angry and disappointed when he arrived back in 2118 it made him determined to get back here somehow. Besides, Hadron's people weren't expecting to find a boy and a dog inside the C-Bean when they summoned it. Apparently Rudy and Spex took them all by surprise, and once Rudy realized Karla was KROB2090 and that she knew how to control the C-Bean, he took her hostage with the penknife, shoved her inside the pod, and made her bring it back here.

Charlie thinks it serves Karla right after she threatened Donald and me in 1918. But strangely enough, I actually feel sorry for her. Charlie says I'm just being soft because I'm related to her. But it's not that. However much what Karla said has upset me, I can't help thinking none of it's her fault. It's my brother's doing really. Karla said herself she didn't want to have anything to do with the C-Bean mission, but he didn't give her a choice.

Last night I fell asleep beside Kit's cot. Mum and Dad said they found me with my arm around the baby when they got back from the

Burneys. I don't remember them carrying me back to my bed. This morning Mum asked me who the black hoodie belonged to. I didn't know what she was talking about at first until Charlie came round and I remembered. He told Mum the hoodie was his. Then he whispered in my ear 'Houston, we have a problem'. It turned out that he'd taken Karla and Rudy to Lady Grange's house last night, and she'd agreed to let them stay there, only instead of going to bed, Rudy helped himself to her bottle of whisky in the night and when Charlie went over this morning, he found Rudy in a drunken stupor. Thankfully Lady Grange wasn't up and Karla hadn't escaped, so Charlie took Rudy up to Old Jim's underground house, gave him a banana and left him to sober up.

The team of marine biologists from Portugal are turning up on the ferry in a couple of hours' time, so Mum and Dad left the house bright and early this morning to get a big welcome lunch ready down at Evaw's offices with Charlie's parents. After lunch Dad says they're going to install a proper sea level marker down by the jetty. I told Dad before he left the house that the marker was completely under water in 2118 and he gave me this worried look like he thinks I've gone completely mad. I hope not, because otherwise we'll never work out what to do about Karla and Rudy. And the C-Bean.

To wind Karla up, Charlie told her this morning that unless she 'spills the beans' as he put it, he would have to put her in Jim's mouldy old hovel too tonight. She reacted really weirdly, probably because she gets claustrophobic in confined spaces. Just the idea of it has made Karla keen to tell us the rest of her story - she's agreed to have another meeting today. I'm not sure I am ready to hear any more yet, but I do want to get to the bottom of everything, and more than anything I want to understand why the whole C-Bean thing happened to us in the first place.

It was Charlie's idea to have the meeting in the C-Bean. He escorted Karla from Lady Grange's house, and Alice used the cardkey to make the C-Bean materialise in the schoolyard while Charlie and Edie went to get Rudy from Old Jim's underground house. When Alice and Karla stepped into the C-Bean, Alice realised that the last time they'd been inside it together was when Karla threatened Alice with a knife and Donald had to intervene to stop her. She was glad Spex was there this time to protect her if Karla tried to do something violent.

However, on this occasion Karla seemed quite calm and contrite, and it occurred to Alice that she must have been thinking about the same event because Karla sat down on the floor and suddenly blurted out a little speech about it.

'I'm sorry I was so unfriendly when we were prisoners together, Alice. I didn't know how much I was allowed to tell you – they didn't brief me about that part properly before I was sent to 2018 – so when you said I'd been talking in my sleep and that I'd mentioned something about Plan B, the only thing I could think to do was stop talking to you altogether. I could not understand why Dad wasn't calling me off the project when things were going so much worse than when the cyborg Dr Foster was here.'

'That's OK,' Alice said, quite taken aback. 'But what exactly is Plan B?'

Karla sighed. 'There's a lot more to what Hadron Services does than simply enabling people to timeshift, Alice. It started off as a totally different kind of project, doing something really positive – they were basically using a prototype C-Bean to bring species of plants and animals from the past that were extinct in the future, so they could breed or grow them again and replenish the planet's gene pool. That was Plan A – bringing live samples forward in time. Dad – I mean Kit – used to joke about it being a kind of reverse Noah's Ark, but its official project name was Operation Seabean – named after those seeds that wash up on beaches sometimes. Dad gave me one once. I think it's called a Mary's Bean. Your mum gave it to him. Anyway, he still gives this little speech to all the new H.S. employees about how their role is to operate like a seabean – bringing the possibility of life from one place to another, in the hope that it will germinate there.'

Alice was pacing round the C-Bean, remembering the Mary's Bean she'd found in her Christmas stocking and given to her mother as a good-luck present the night before her brother was born. She wondered if it was the same one that Karla now had. She suddenly felt quite upset and needed to change the subject.

'Why did they call the time-travel device a "C-Bean" with a C, and not "Seabean"?'

'Because the default timeshift period was set to 100 years, so Dad's boss came up with the idea of "C-Bean" – the letter C is the Roman numeral for a hundred – so it's basically a "bean" or pod that can travel 100 years through time.'

'Cool, I like that,' Alice said, wiping her eyes. Then she remembered her original question.

'You still haven't told me what Plan B is, Karla.'

'OK. Here goes … When the public got to know about the new animal species arriving from the past, Dad's boss started getting requests from people who wanted to go backwards in time. But they'd done some research that showed it could be bad for your health, as well as messing around with the time sequence. They ran a load of tests, sending mice back and forth in time, which confirmed the risks but it got them into a whole lot of trouble with the Animal Protection League. A year later the International Senate passed a worldwide law making it illegal to go back in time. That wasn't just because of the health risks, but also because they realised the more people that went back in time, the more it was just going to create problems in the past – I mean in your time.'

'And did that make them stop?'

'Nowhere near – the threat of imprisonment and severe illness was never going to be enough to stop people wanting to timeshift. Once Dad's boss realised he had a huge number of customers willing to pay a hefty price tag to timeshift back to a better time, he cashed in. That was the start of Plan B, and it's when the C-Bean project turned into something much less noble. They have a waiting list of over a hundred thousand people now,' Karla paused.

'And what about the crates we saw in El Dorado, marked "Operation Seabean"? There were loads of fake animals there. Are they that part of Plan B, too?'

'You weren't supposed to go there – to Brazil, I mean. Looking back, I blame El Dorado for everything – Kit was basically a good man and a talented scientist and then he went to work for the wrong guys,' Karla said knowingly, pushing her glasses back up her nose. She paused. Alice was looking at her doubtfully, waiting for more of an explanation.

'People get very desperate and devious when there's not enough to go round, Alice. You've seen for yourself already how much damage has been done to the world's ecological balance in 2118 – the climate has changed massively everywhere. With so many countries flooded, the places that aren't underwater are hopelessly overcrowded. Food is a real issue. People are starving and getting ill…'

'Like St Kilda in the olden days…' said Alice.

'Exactly. It was all over the news when St Kilda was evacuated for the second time, exactly a hundred years later in 2030 during World War III, for the same reasons as in 1930 – because people were starving, getting ill and dying. By 2110, it was happening the world over – and people would do anything just to stay alive – you name it, looting, killing, fighting. There were tribes all over the place smuggling gold, bees, food and water illegally. And, in Dad's case, trafficking animals and humans as well. Kit's done a bit of all of it in his time.'

'You make my brother sound like a pirate.'

'Well, he is. Especially once he started working at Øbsidon.'

Alice's head was starting to reel.

'Øbsidon. OK, slow down, Karla. That's something else you need to fill me in on – Spex has "Øbsidon" engraved on his collar. Look!' Alice bent down and showed Karla the gold-and-black disk.

'Is James Ferguson something to do with Øbsidon?' continued Alice. 'He mentioned it a few times in his notebooks – isn't it some kind of flammable material he once invented? Ever since our house caught fire, I've been wondering if Øbsidon was the black rubbery stuff they put on the back of the C-Bean Mark 4 cardkey and if that's what made the fire start. What do you know about it, Karla? You've got to tell me! Is the C-Bean owned by Øbsidon? Charlie and I read something about a factory in China – is that where Øbsidon is made?' Alice stopped in full flow, breathless and dizzy all of a sudden. Karla paused, studying Alice's face.

'You saw what was in James' notebooks?'

Alice nodded and Karla looked quite shocked.

'Maybe if you want all of this to make sense, we actually need to go there and meet him,' Karla mused out loud.

'Go where? Meet who? My brother?'

'No, Foster.'

Sensing that Alice was starting to feel frantic and perhaps realising that

Karla needed a little help in explaining everything, the C-Bean began singing the sea shanty to her, and its white walls became a sort of photo album of images of someone with white curly hair in a lab coat, who looked exactly like their old teacher, smiling into the camera as he posed with various pairs of animals: badgers, crocodiles, eagles, gorillas, leopards, turtles, monkeys, iguanas, penguins, wolves.

'I thought Foster was a cyborg. Is that him in the pictures with animals that have been imported to the future as part of Plan A?' Alice asked, staring at the walls in awe.

'Yes and no.'

'What do you mean?'

'The man in the pictures, who you recognise as Dr Foster, your old teacher – and who does indeed look exactly like the cyborg Hadron Services sent back to 2018 – is actually the real Dr Foster.'

'I still don't get it. Who is he?'

'He's the real person on whom your teacher – the cyborg – was based, or copied from, if you will. The real Dr Foster was Dad's boss and mentor for many years. He's the C-Bean's real designer – not me. He's also the guy in charge of Øbsidon and the person who set up Operation Seabean and subsequently Plan B.'

'I see. So where is the real Dr Foster now?'

'It depends what you mean by "now", Alice. In 2018, of course, he is not yet born. In my now – 2118 – he has been dead for eight years…' Karla's voice trailed off.

'Listen, Alice – maybe this isn't such a disaster, after all.' Karla stood up and starting cleaning her glasses. 'When Rudy kidnapped me, I thought it couldn't get any worse, but you've just given me an idea. You could put a stop to all this. You could put an end to Plan B for good – confront Dr Foster in person and convince him that what he's doing is wrong. Think about it – if we allow people from the future to go back 100 years, it'll create even more pressure on the earth's limited resources in your time. The sheer impact of that extra burden of human population will make climate change escalate totally out of control. The earth will be completely uninhabitable within just a few decades.' Karla put her glasses back on and blinked at Alice.

'Hang on, Karla. I still don't get the connection between Kit and the real Dr Foster.'

'Foster was an entrepreneur – some say a genius. He developed a time-travel algorithm and built the first C-Bean using a revolutionary material he'd invented called Øbsidon. When he died, he left the formula for it to Dad in his will. Dad refined the formula and brought out the C-Bean Mark 4, using a new isotope of Øbsidon in its construction. It gave the C-Bean more advanced functionality but it also became much more dangerous and unstable. Quite apart from being flammable, as you found out, the discomfort people started experiencing when they were being timeshifted is likely to have disastrous long-term genetic consequences unless they are treated in good time.'

Alice gulped, remembering how she'd allowed their C-Bean Mark 3 to be upgraded to a Mark 4, and the unpleasant feeling of being rearranged she'd experienced when they travelled in it ever since. She didn't even want to consider the consequences it had already had on her own body.

'Right, let me get a few things straight. Does my brother work for El Dorado, Øbsidon or Hadron Services?'

'It's complicated, Alice.'

Karla sat down on the floor again.

'Kit went to work for El Dorado in 2089. About ten years later the real Dr Foster, who was a major shareholder in El Dorado, spotted how talented Dad was and persuaded him to go and work for him at Øbsidon HQ in China. By the time Foster died in 2110, timeshifting had been made illegal, so in order to carry on as a business, Dad set up Hadron Services to continue their work. That's when he relocated the whole operation to St Kilda, to keep his timeshifting work well hidden. He knew that Evaw's underwater research facility was still intact and it didn't take much to overhaul it to run it as a pirate base – a black ops site, if you will.'

'I see,' said Alice slowly, finally discovering the connection between the C-Bean and her island home. She was leaning against one wall and staring at the ceiling.

'I think I get the picture now, but how does James Ferguson fit into it? How come his notebooks were full of stuff about the C-Bean and Øbsidon too?'

'James was working with Foster before Foster recruited Dad. In fact they never actually met – Dad and James, I mean. James was Foster's first business partner – when they started working together, they were separated in time by a century. Basically, Foster was in 2058 sending messages to James in 1958 about his early version of the time-travel algorithm using some elementary messaging technology.'

'The instant mailboat drawer?'

'Yes – that's how they communicated to begin with. Wow, Alice. Do you know about that, too?'

Alice nodded. 'Go on,' she urged.

'Foster sent James his designs for a prototype C-Bean that way and James built one and started sending live samples to Foster in the future. Initially he could only send small stuff like insects, birds' eggs, butterflies, moss, wild flowers – things he'd collected on St Kilda. They knew Plan A was going to be a success when James sent a pair of live puffins to 2059 and they raised a family of chicks in an artificial burrow that Foster set up for them.'

'Then what?'

'After James' dad died in 1960...'

'You mean Donald Ferguson?'

'Yes, Donald. James decided to risk transporting himself to the future – to 2060 – in order to work on the next phase of Plan A with Foster. They did that right up until 2077 and then, one night, James suddenly vanished. Foster always maintained that James had somehow gone back to his own time, but at that stage the C-Bean Mark 1's timeshift function was not advanced enough to enable any living things to go backwards in time. So it was a real mystery how James got away and where he went. It left Foster without a business partner, and he struggled on by himself for a few years, until he recruited Dad. Dad thinks Foster never told him the whole story about what happened with James, but there was obviously some kind of breakdown in trust between James and Foster.'

'I see,' Alice said, mulling over all the pieces to what felt like a vast jigsaw puzzle. She was running her fingers over the wall of the C-Bean and creating a complex pattern of colours and interlocking lines. When she stopped, the C-Bean seemed to take what she had drawn and turn it into a moving kaleidoscope of music and maths, playing gently in the background and constantly changing. Karla watched for a while as the shapes changed and merged together. She sighed.

'You know, Alice, Dad told me recently that if James hadn't disappeared in 2077, Dad would never have gone to work for Øbsidon. None of this would have happened. I am so angry with him – he knew it wasn't safe for people to go backwards in time, even with the Mark 3. But he went ahead with it anyway. With his own family members! You and me! We're Hadron Services' guinea pigs, Alice! I had no idea what would happen when we did the reset and it sent us back in time by 100 years. Then, next thing I knew, you and Donald insisted on taking us all back to 1851 on some pointless trip to that crystal palace. And now, to top it all, that delinquent kid Rudy made me travel back in time yet again. I'm going to get sick, I know I am!'

At that point, Karla started sobbing uncontrollably, which made Spex start to paw the door to get out of the C-Bean.

'Yes, for God's sake open the door, Alice – I'm feeling so claustrophobic in here!'

Alice opened the C-Bean and Spex ran outside. Charlie and Edie were walking across the schoolyard towards her, trying to control Rudy, who was still rolling drunk.

As they reached the C-Bean, Rudy blurted out, 'I happy boy Rudy today!' and was promptly sick on the grass outside the door.

'I'm pleased to hear it, Rudy. Come inside – you're just in time, guys,' replied Alice.

'In time for what? Rudy's in no fit state for anything,' Edie advised, producing a tissue for him to wipe his mouth. Rudy let out a loud burp. 'See what I mean?'

'OK, but we have some more important things to deal with than Rudy's hangover,' Alice said bluntly.

'Like what?'

'Karla's been filling me in on a few things, and thinks we need to confront the C-Bean's real inventor – the person in fact who invented time travel – the real Dr Foster. He's behind everything – none of this would have happened if it wasn't for him, and Karla says he's about to exploit the power of time travel for all the wrong reasons. It's up to us to stop him before it becomes an utter disaster.'

'Whoever this guy Foster really is, and whatever he's up to, the answer is simple Alice – No way.'

'Edie, I'm begging you!' Karla wailed, 'This is important. He's a very determined scientist. Please let's make him stop what he's doing before it's too late! I'm only asking that you come with me in the C-Bean to visit Dr Foster at Øbsidon HQ before he goes ahead with Plan B.'

'I'm not going anywhere ever again in this thing, and that's a fact,' announced Edie. 'And I'm not falling for your story, Karla – as far as I'm concerned, you've been lying to us right from the start and if you believe a word she's saying, Alice, you're an idiot. It's all just one big wind-up. She doesn't even bother putting on her fake German accent anymore. I was only here for the meeting, so you can let me out right now.' Edie looked defiantly at Karla, who just shrugged and turned away.

The C-Bean's door opened and she stepped out. Alice could see Spix flying around outside. The parrot flew down to perch on Edie's shoulder for a moment, looking at her quizzically.

'Don't look at me like that, Spix. I'm the only one with any sense around here.'

But Spix didn't want to miss out on another adventure, so when Edie started to walk home, he flew inside the C-Bean and blurted out a loud 'Olá!'

'*Olá, olá, olá, olá!*' hollered a drunken Rudy at the top of his voice, teetering around, his yellow eyes bleary and unfocused.

'Shut up, Rudy,' Charlie said, grabbing his shoulder and making him sit down on the floor of the C-Bean. Spex started licking Rudy's face and making him giggle uncontrollably. Alice started sniggering.

'OK, that's the funny bit over. So what's the real story?' asked Charlie, hands on hips.

'I'm not lying. Not now, anyway,' Karla said quietly.

'Go on,' Charlie urged.

'I had to lie about who I was the first time I was sent back to 2018 or the mission wouldn't have worked at all. You had to think I really was the C-Bean's inventor who'd come over from Germany to help you fix your mobile classroom. You would never have known any different if I hadn't got stuck in 1918 when we reset this stupid thing, and then you found my fake passport. But I'm telling you the truth now, Alice. Honestly.'

Alice nodded. 'So when exactly do we need to arrive in the future to confront Dr Foster?'

'Ideally, just before James Ferguson left in 2077. That's when we'd stand the best chance of convincing Foster,' Karla replied.

Alice remembered from James' notebooks and the internet research she and Charlie had done that James was nominated for a Nobel Peace Prize in 1977, so what Karla was saying made sense – he must have somehow travelled back to his own time around then.

'And where exactly are we going to find him?' Charlie said.

'Øbsidon HQ.'

Alice could hear Edie's voice pestering her in the back of her mind, and had a feeling that maybe Edie was right. Should they all step outside the C-Bean now and just let Karla and Rudy go back to 2118, and then the whole thing would be over with? But Alice was aware of an even stronger feeling that, even if they did that, it would not be over – there would just be further complications.

'OK, Charlie, are you up for this?' Alice asked, a little warily.

'Right now I'm up for anything that will keep Karla, Rudy and the C-Bean from being discovered, because I don't think we could pull off any more bizarre explanations, Alice,' Charlie sighed.

Rudy had fallen asleep in the corner, with Spex curled up beside him.

'In that case, let's do it.'

'Thank you, Alice!' said Karla, her voice full of grateful relief.

'Don't thank me till it's over,' Alice said as she closed the door and instructed the C-Bean to take them to Øbsidon HQ on 18 September 2077. But the C-Bean seemed unable to produce the exact coordinates and instead showed a map of the general area where it presumed it was located, in the south of China. It added one short piece of information: 'Øbsidon Futures® (Ø.F.) registered 2098, CEO Dr Adrian Foster'.

'Where is Øbsidon's HQ, Karla? Why isn't it coming up?' Alice asked.

'Wasn't it listed as one of the test sites before, Alice? Remember, it said "Ø.F."'

'It's been blocked now. Hadron must suspect. Look, trust me. I'm going right out on a limb here, and Dad would kill me if he knew I was doing this,' Karla said conspiratorially. 'But I happen to know that although Øbsidon's whereabouts is classified, there is a guide who can get us there.'

In the absence of a precise location for Øbsidon HQ, Alice instructed the C-Bean to use the coordinates for Charlie's grandparents' tower block, Harbourside Tower 6, from their last visit to Hong Kong. Just before they arrived, the C-Bean announced that oxygen levels would be acceptable for human life at their destination, and they promptly landed on the roof of the skyscraper, just like the previous time. But Hong Kong in 2077 was not quite how Alice remembered it. Even before they set foot outside the C-Bean, she could hear a hammering sound on the roof and when they emerged there was a fierce autumn monsoon in progress. As they stepped out, curtains of hot acid rain were plummeting onto the roof of the building and evaporating on contact into swirling clouds of vapour, the wind stirring it all up together with shards of metal and other debris. The rain stung their skin and a piece of debris struck Charlie on his head, which started bleeding. Spix was swept up in a ferocious gust, and for several tense minutes seemed unable to fly out of the maelstrom. Eventually, Rudy was able to hook him down using what remained of a lightning conductor rod that he found lying on the roof near an exit hatch.

'Quick, let's get down below and out of the storm,' Alice shouted, tugging at the hatch.

When they climbed through it and down to the floor below, they could see that the building was abandoned and in a bad state of repair. The only thing working was some emergency lighting, which kept flickering on and off. There was obviously not enough power left in the building to make the lifts work, so they walked down the escape stairs to Charlie's granddad's apartment on the 30th floor. They found the door to the apartment wide open. Spex trotted straight in, following a trail he'd picked up. By the look of the mess, someone had obviously been through the contents and taken anything valuable or edible. Charlie's family's beautiful grey plush carpet and elegant antique furniture were long gone, with bare concrete floors in their place, and vestiges of the last occupants' silk wallpaper still clung to the damp walls in places.

'Looters,' Rudy observed grimly.

'Come on, let's go. There's no point in staying here,' Charlie scoffed, looking round in dismay.

They walked down 30 storeys in silence. Some of the steps were broken and there were gaps where the balustrades and handrails were missing. Alice followed Karla, Rudy and Charlie down, wondering what kind of scene would greet them when they reached the lobby. The storm seemed to have subsided but, as they came to the last flight of stairs, they all stopped. It appeared that the marble steps disappeared into a lake of murky water that filled the last few metres of the emergency stairwell. The dog pushed past them to investigate something he'd spied in the water, but Spix had the opposite reaction and suddenly became quite agitated. He flung himself at the windows, desperately looking for a way out. Alice peered outside through the dirty plate-glass windows. Where the street had once been, with its crowded pavements and tangle of overhead tram wires and telegraph cables, was now a vast canal. It looked like pictures she'd seen of Venice, water flowing between all the buildings.

In the gathering twilight, the only signs of any human activity Alice could see were a couple of boats tethered to lampposts. Charlie waded in chest-deep and started swimming towards one of the boats. He turned and beckoned to the others. Spex launched himself into the water and was paddling over to Charlie. Spix clung to Alice's collarbone until they were out through the door. The water didn't smell too good and there were dark, indeterminate objects floating around in it, but it was cooler than the stifling air temperature, so Alice actually found it quite a relief to have to swim over to the boat.

There was a large fan-like motor at the stern and a solar panel taped onto the front deck.

There was also some kind of pole lying in the bottom of its hull.

'We need to get a move on before someone comes back for it,' Karla warned as they hauled themselves aboard.

'Where's Rudy?' Alice asked.

Rudy was standing up to his neck in the water on the other side of the street, looking scared stiff.

Charlie was trying to work out how to connect the starter cable to get the rotary blades working. Suddenly he managed to start the motor and the boat sprang to life.

'Which way?'

'North. But first we need to go down to the old harbour. That's where we'll find a guide,' Karla advised.

The boat drifted towards Rudy, who flung himself across the stern when they got close. Somehow the movement caused by his clambering aboard made the engine shift up a gear and the blades start turning slowly. Once Rudy had settled on a seat, he noticed that there was a taped-up break in the cable that connected the motor to the solar panel. He gripped the join and the blades speeded up immediately.

'Must be a loose connection, but we can't see in the dark well enough to fix it. Keep hold of that cable, buddy,' Charlie muttered to Rudy. 'Alice, you steer. It looks like Spix and Spex are our lookouts.'

It was true – the dog and the parrot were both sitting motionless on the foredeck, eyes trained on the water ahead of them. Alice moved to the back of the boat and manoeuvred the boat to head towards the place she remembered the harbour to be. She steered a course down the very street where last time there had been a night market and, as she rounded the corner at the end of the street, she remembered the spot where she'd bought a large spiky durian fruit from a street seller. It all seemed so long ago, like another world.

The harbour was bigger than Alice remembered, until she realised that the sea now came up higher than the old harbour wall and had flooded the surrounding dockside. Mounted on a pontoon floating on the water was a little wooden cabin with a light in the window. Karla pointed to it.

'That's where we'll find our guide,' she said.

Alice waited in the boat with Rudy and the animals, while Karla and Charlie climbed out onto the pontoon and went inside the cabin to enquire about the guide.

Charlie appeared a few minutes later. 'It's no good,' he said. 'They want payment in gold, and we don't have any.'

'Gold?'

'Yeah, real solid gold. They made it sound as if everyone just walks around with heaps of it in their pockets these days.'

'Maybe people do in 2077 – you heard what they were making in El Dorado.'

Rudy started undoing the collar from around Spex's neck. He detached the gold-and-black 'Øbsidon' disk and handed it to Charlie.

'Here. Is Gold.'

Charlie took the disk, turning it over in his palm. 'You reckon this is real gold, mate?' He chuckled. 'OK. I'll give it a try.'

Moments later, a wizened old woman came out of the cabin. She was dressed in faded dungarees with a headscarf wound around her head and she was sucking on something that had stained her lips and chin dark red.

'Where you get?' she held up the disk and peered at Alice. Alice just shrugged. The woman tutted, and pocketed the disk.

'Øbsidon is bad place, is in DeeZee. Dangerous place,' she grumbled, but was nevertheless clambering into their boat and pointing out which way they should be heading.

'What's DeeZee?' Alice asked Karla. But it was Rudy who replied.

'DeeZee mean Dead Zone. Nothing grow. No life. All dead.'

'And Øbsidon, what exactly is it?'

Karla cleared her throat to speak.

'Øbsidon's a fortress. It's Dr Foster's answer to the Dead Zone. Technically it's an experimental biome. They built it as an artificial habitat so they could breed and nurture all the creatures they imported from the past.'

'So basically it's a giant greenhouse?' Alice asked, remembering the Great Exhibition with its huge glass structures and the elm trees inside that she'd visited with Donald in 1851.

'Yes, something like that – it's a climate-controlled environment that perfectly replicates tropical conditions found on earth a century or more ago. As far as I know, it's the only one of its kind in the world. From what I can remember about Plan A from my training, by 2077 they were just starting to populate the biome with larger species of mammal. Which is fortunate for us, because I reckon the only way we'll get inside Foster's fortress is to offer to trade with him.'

'Trade what? We've given our only piece of gold to this boat woman,' Charlie pointed out.

'We have something they want more than gold, Charlie,' said Karla tentatively.

'Huh?'

'Live specimens.'

'You mean we offer ourselves as trade? Are they populating this biome with live children?' Charlie joked.

'Not us, Charlie. I mean Spix and Spex.'

Alice looked at Karla in horror. Had she been lied to after all?

'I'm not giving our animals up, Karla, no way! Spex has been experimented on enough as it is in Hadron's lab, and who knows what happened to Spix in El Dorado before we found him again there!' she said. Spex had pricked up his ears and edged closer to Alice when he heard his name mentioned. Spix responded by fluffing out his chest feathers and chirping loudly 'Spix-Spex, Spix-Spex'.

But no one laughed.

'I don't see how else we're going to gain admittance into the compound any other way, Alice. It's impossible,' Karla retorted in a high, defiant tone, the muscle in her jaw continuously twitching. Everyone fell silent.

The solar battery only lasted about an hour, long enough to get the boat north of the city before it got dark. They were heading up a narrow channel that led inland through a vast mangrove swamp when the engine cut out. Alice looked around. The trees surrounding them were long since dead and the heat was more intense than ever. Everything was silent apart from a low droning buzz, which they realised was coming from a dense, moving cloud up ahead. As they got closer Alice realised that it was not mist but a swarm of large, long-legged insects feasting on what looked like a dead animal, its bloated belly protruding from the water.

Suddenly the old woman started muttering something under her breath that sounded like 'mung, mung!' She rummaged in the pockets of her dungarees and pulled out some incense sticks. When she lit them and gave one to each of the children, Rudy suddenly seemed to understand what she was saying and went rigid with fear.

'Mung!' he repeated and, without warning, suddenly stood up in the boat, making it rock violently from side to side and veer off course.

'What's the matter, Rudy? What is "mung"?' asked Alice.

'It's Cantonese slang for mosquito,' Karla whispered. 'I've heard they all carry malaria around here. Rudy, sit down and stay still,' Karla urged. Rudy flashed her a look, his yellow eyes glinting with fear in the dark.

'Don't want get sick! Happen before.'

The swarm had detected the scent of fresh human flesh in the boat and was coming towards them. The woman leaned over the side of the boat and used her arms to try to turn it around and move back down the channel, but the insects were in their hair, noses and eyes within seconds.

Alice felt herself drift slowly into unconsciousness, the malarial organisms from copious mosquito bites pulsing through her veins. She lay still in the boat, dimly aware of Spex licking her face, but everything else was foggy. She could sense the others going slack around her, as they too fell victim to the attack. All except the old woman, who somehow pulled the pole out from under them and took charge. With a burning incense stick gripped between her teeth for protection, the woman peered into the darkness, still sucking on the red seeds. As if guided by some inner compass, she let the pole slide into the water until it touched the bottom, pushed off and continued north towards the Øbsidon compound.

When Alice awoke she felt swollen, feverish and itchy. In the pale dawn light, she could see mosquito bites covering her arms and legs, every one a raised red blister the size of a saucer. They were still in the boat, Rudy and Charlie lying awkwardly back-to-back next to each other. Karla was curled up in a ball at the front, her face pallid and her lips blue.

All around the boat, the seawater was grey, inert and polluted with occasional pieces of rotting organic matter floating among degraded plastic containers. The sun's early-morning rays skated across the surface, piercing the translucent objects nearest to the boat, making the detritus look almost beautiful for a moment. So this was the Dead Zone – one vast sterile expanse, ruined forever by humankind. The old woman pulled in the pole and let the boat drift. Shielding her eyes from the low sun, she peered at the islands up ahead. Spex yawned and whined softly in Alice's lap. The parrot, meanwhile, clung to her shoulder and was watching the old woman's every move.

'I'm starving,' Charlie groaned as he woke, obviously forgetting their predicament. He pushed Rudy over onto his front and eased himself up into a sitting position.

'You lucky,' said the old woman. 'Øbsidon only place make own food. Almost there, look!' she said, pointing ahead.

They were approaching an island that appeared to be surrounded by a high fence whose posts stood in the water. Beyond the fence, Alice could see what looked like a giant soap bubble enclosing the whole island, its glassy surface reflecting the pinks and oranges in the sky. Foster's biome.

The old woman had brought the boat to within 20 metres of the line of fence posts when Alice suddenly felt an electrical charge ripple across her skin. She let go of Spix and Spex and clutched her arm in terror.

'The fence. It must be electrified,' Charlie said in a tense whisper.

'Yes. But not water,' the old woman grunted. 'You kids swim rest of way. Keep heads under all way to shore,' she advised, waving her arm to demonstrate that they needed to exit the boat quickly. Rudy was still asleep, so she poked him hard in the ribs with her foot to wake him. He woke with a start, his yellow eyes blazing, ready to confront whoever had kicked him, until he realised it was the old woman.

'C'mon, out now, boys and girls!' she urged. 'Take goods with you. Hurry! Øbsidon watching us. Don't want be seen!' She seemed quite anxious to get going and had untied her headscarf to drape it over her face so she would not be recognised. Charlie pointed out the surveillance cameras mounted on the top of each of the fence posts. In the distance, the Øbsidon biome suddenly looked totally impenetrable.

Alice was the first to slip over the side of the boat and into the warm, dirty water. She had no idea how long she could hold her breath for, and the island still looked quite some distance away. Charlie followed, and as he lowered his torso into the water, Spix took off, wheeling up into the sky and squawking his usual mantra '*Perigroso, perigroso!*' Sensing the bird's panic, Spex barked and splashed in beside Alice, paddling rapidly towards the shore. Alice realised she would have to push the dog's head under when they got in line with the electric fence to avoid him being electrocuted. Meanwhile, Rudy sat in the boat, refusing to move. No matter what the old woman said to him, he just shook his head. Finally he admitted, 'No swim. Not knowhow.'

'Karla, come on – you're going to have to help him,' Alice called, treading water and pushing the rubbish on the surface out of her way. But Karla just shook her head.

'I'm not coming with you.'

'What?' Alice spluttered, nearly swallowing some of the water.

'You have to do this on your own, Alice. I'm allergic to everything inside there.'

'Well, thanks for not telling us earlier, Karla!' Charlie said angrily as he grabbed one side of the boat and somehow managed to manoeuvre Rudy into the water with them. Alice swam across and got hold of Rudy's other arm. The old woman started arguing with Karla when she realised she wasn't getting out of the boat. Karla said something in Cantonese, pulled up her hood and the woman turned the boat round and started heading back the way they'd come.

Alice was trying her best not to panic. It was taking all her effort to make sure none of the dirty water got into her nose or mouth, and she still had to keep Rudy afloat. She could feel her legs tiring before they were even halfway to the shore. Spex had swum on ahead, out of reach. Alice grabbed something that was floating on the water and threw it to Spex, shouting 'Fetch'. Thankfully the item plunged under the surface and Spex dived after it, reappearing on the other side of the line of electrified fencing. Alice could feel the charge on her skin again and knew it was time for her to go under, too. She closed her eyes, took a deep breath and sank down into the filthy grey water, dragging Rudy with her and trying to judge how many strokes she needed to make before she was clear of the fence above. She could feel Rudy's legs instinctively kicking against her as he struggled to reach the surface. She held his arm tightly and uttered a silent and fervent wish that they would all make it safely to dry land. It was only when they resurfaced on the inside of the perimeter fence that Alice noticed that Rudy was now swimming by himself without realising it. She let go of his arm and watched as he splashed towards the shore.

'Rudy, we made it – you can do it!' He beamed at her and kept up his frantic paddle until the water was shallow enough to stand up.

Spix was waiting for them, perched on a rock that looked like it was streaked with veins of melted plastic the same colour as his blue feathers. He eyed the humans nervously as they squeezed out their clothes. Spex shook himself dry, barked and bounded off, following a vivid scent trail that led off the beach and into a scrubland of black thorny bushes. It looked as if there had been a fire – the bushes were in fact not black but burned, and the ground was scorched and cracked. The children followed the dog in single file, unsure where the trail was leading. Up ahead, the glass biome loomed over them, and Alice could now see a dense jungle inside reaching right up to the top of the dome, hundreds of different kinds of trees, flowers and creepers all competing for sunlight.

Spex brought them to a place where the scorched terrain had been dug away to form a cutting that led deep into the ground beneath the biome. At the bottom of the cutting there was a kind of cage surrounding entrance gates. There was a sign beside the gates stating 'Goods Inwards', next to an entry keypad similar to the one for the airlock on St Kilda in 2118. Alice began to wonder if Rudy's dead finger would work here too. She looked at him.

'The finger, Rudy?'

Rudy nodded and produced the gruesome item from his pocket, placing it on the keypad.

No response.

Then they heard a click and a voice said, 'Enter UAT to enable us to identify your goods.'

'What's a UAT?' asked Charlie. 'Some kind of password?'

'It's that serial number the cloned parrots in El Dorado had under their tails, remember. I don't think either Spex or Spix have one…' Alice sighed with disappointment.

She thought for a moment, trying to remember the inscription on the gold disk. When Spex had reappeared with it around his neck, she assumed it was because someone had given him a new name – but what if it was, in fact, a code?

'Wait, I've got it.'

She wiped the sweat off her forehead and slowly typed the letters 'B-O-R-K' into the keypad.

The gate clicked open so faintly that Alice thought at first she had imagined it. She picked up Spex and tucked him under her arm before walking through the cage and into the biome. The atmosphere inside was pleasantly warm and steamy. Spix flew off high above them, swooping and squawking in sheer delight as he discovered his favourite nut hanging from one of the tropical trees. It was obviously a close approximation of his native environment. Alice could hear a stream trickling through the undergrowth and, as she got closer to it, she noticed something floating in the crystal-clear water. It was a seabean. She bent down and fished it out of the stream, holding it dripping wet in her palm. She felt sure it was a sign that she was getting closer to finding out the truth.

'Look, Alice – there are durians growing in here!' Charlie was staring up at the spiky fruit hanging overhead. Alice gazed in awe at this lush and verdant scene and saw that it was alive with butterflies, dragonflies, grasshoppers and tree frogs.

'Look – Bee too,' said Rudy, smiling as he watched a small swarm flying in and out of a hive hanging from a branch above his head.

'Come on, guys – this isn't a nature lesson,' Charlie urged them as he scratched his mosquito bites.

'But that's exactly what this is!' a voice said, seemingly from nowhere. 'Welcome, my friends, step this way.'

Alice looked up and noticed a high-level walkway, suspended in the treetops and running around the perimeter of the biome. A man with curly white hair wearing a lab coat appeared to be waiting for them there. She knew straight away they were in the presence of the real Dr Foster.

D r Foster led them to a large wooden villa with deep overhanging eaves in the middle of the biome. At the entrance, he asked them to remove their shoes, and then ushered them into a beautiful room lined with bamboo panels overlooking a garden. The floor was covered in soft woven matting and strewn with silk cushions. Alice and Charlie sat on the cushions and waited while Dr Foster stepped out of the room for a moment. Alice realised that she felt nervous. She was worrying about where Spix and Spex were, and her bites were driving her crazy, but she didn't dare scratch them. The only things to ease her sense of discomfort were the fans blowing cool air over their damp clothes. Rudy kept walking restlessly around the room, opening and shutting various glass cabinets displaying a collection of various black rocks. It reminded Alice of the display cases she'd seen in the American Museum of Natural History in New York.

'Rudy, don't touch anything,' Alice hissed.

'I see you like my little museum,' Dr Foster observed when he returned.

'Sorry, Dr Foster. He doesn't mean to be rude. What are all those rocks, exactly?' enquired Alice politely.

'It is my father's collection. They are more than just rocks; they're meteorites – fragments from a very old, very large meteor that crashed into the Earth in northern Russia in 2042. Father discovered that they had the strangest properties. I think you will find them most interesting. Watch this.'

Dr Foster opened one cabinet and took out a particularly uninteresting lump of black rock and gave it to Charlie. As he handled it, the whole rock changed colour and became a vivid sky blue.

'Son, the specimen you are holding came from Outer Space. It has time-travelled many hundreds of thousands of light years. All the energy from its time travel is encoded in its chemistry at a sub-atomic level. It's what I used to derive Øbsidon. You see, Øbsidon is not just the name of my company, but also the name I gave to my most important invention to date – a powerful patented material that exploits the same molecular structure as this meteorite. Without it, Operation Seabean could not exist because, you see, it is the very thing that enables my C-Bean device to time travel.'

Charlie handed the rock to Rudy, whereupon it changed colour again, becoming a fiery reddish-orange. When it was completely orange, Rudy suddenly dropped it.

'Burn Hands. Very hot!' he exclaimed.

'Ah yes, in the wrong hands, its thermopower is also activated. We are working on a fix for that right now.' Dr Foster bent down and picked up the rock and beckoned to Alice. 'You have a try, my dear.'

Alice reluctantly took the rock, holding it with her fingers wide apart, ready to let go should it become scalding hot again. But instead the rock turned a deep translucent green and then became virtually invisible. Charlie and Rudy watched, transfixed. Alice noticed that even Dr Foster looked dumbstruck.

'How very interesting, my friend. You appear to have a unique power over this little rock.' He stared quizzically at Alice for a moment. She felt embarrassed, so she placed the invisible rock back inside the cabinet beside its identification card, marked 'Øbsidon Mark 3'. As she closed the cabinet door, she could that see the rock was already reappearing, just like the C-Bean had reappeared when they were at the Great Exhibition in 1851.

A door slid open behind them and a dark-haired girl about ten years old, who Dr Foster addressed as Rachel, brought in a pot of jasmine tea and some delicate porcelain cups and set them down on a low black table. Dr Foster proceeded to pour the tea with great care. Alice watched him carefully and studied his face – he looked exactly like their old teacher, but his movements as he handed out the cups seemed to be more smooth and natural. Then she saw that, when he picked up the teapot, the heat left a blue circular mark on the table. Her own cup did the same.

'Is the table made of Øbsidon too, Dr Foster?

'Yes, naturally. Now, please, try the tea. I am very proud. It has been made with our first flush of jasmine, pollinated by real insects. So it is, technically, the first real tea that has been produced in over fifty years. I hope you like it.'

Alice noticed that his voice, with its gentle Asian inflections, also sounded more natural and authentic than the cyborg Dr Foster's American drawl. She took a sip of the tea. The others did likewise. The warm aromatic liquid tasted exquisite. There was a long pause, during which Alice felt a sense of calm descend. She was so relaxed that, before she realised what she was doing, she found herself making a direct proposal to their host.

'Dr Foster, I can see that your Operation Seabean is a great success. We have recently arrived in Hong Kong and would like to offer something we hope will add to your project – an, um, unusual breed of dog from New York and a rare Spix's Macaw that we rescued from a recent trip to the Amazon.'

'Is that so? But please, we will talk business in due course, my dear. For now, I suggest you rest and recuperate from your travels. Later I would like to show you more of our work before we enter negotiations. You must all be tired. Rachel will show you to your lodgings. You can bathe, change your clothes, relax. Leave your specimens with me – their value to us will be assessed in due course.'

Dr Foster pressed a bell to summon someone. Alice stared helplessly when a lab technician appeared with Spex and Spix in two cardboard boxes.

The technician showed them briefly to Dr Foster and said something to him in Cantonese before carrying them off. Charlie gave Alice a sharp dig in the shin but all she could do was stare helplessly after them.

'So, it is agreed. We will meet at sundown for dinner in the Great Hall when we will be joined by my business partner, Rachel's father, and we shall be delighted to hear your proposal then.'

Rachel took them down a wide passageway and into a side wing of the villa, where several rooms opened off a central courtyard. In the middle of the courtyard was a beautiful water sculpture made of Øbsidon that changed by itself from black to gold to invisible and back again as the water in rivulets ran over its smooth surface. Rachel led them around the edge of the courtyard and slid back a paper screen to reveal the main room. There were beds unrolled on the floor for each of them and lying on top of each bed was a quilt, a folded silk robe and a pair of silk slippers.

'Papa made all the silk himself – with imported silkworms,' Rachel informed them, smiling shyly.

'It's beautiful,' Alice said, kneeling down to touch the soft fabric. 'I'm Alice. Do you live here, Rachel?'

'Yes, with my papa, James Ferguson. You will meet him later.'

'Of course,' said Alice with a sharp intake of breath, realising that, in the past few months, she had met not only this girl's father but also her grandfather, Donald, and her great-grandmother, Dora.

'I look forward to meeting him,' she said lamely, at a loss as to what else to say.

'The bathrooms are through that way.' Rachel was pointing to another doorway to the left of a large bookcase.

'Will our animals be well treated? I am quite concerned,' Alice questioned her further.

'All our animals are well cared for. Would you like to see our newest arrivals before dinner? They came yesterday – we have two baby pandas. Papa gave them to me as a gift for my birthday. I'm their keeper,' Rachel said with a certain amount of pride.

'Pandas?' Charlie asked, incredulous.

'Yes. I will come back for you in an hour, to show you.' And with that, Rachel bowed politely and withdrew. Charlie waited until she had gone before he laid into Alice with a volley of criticisms.

'Brilliant performance back there with Foster, Alice – absolutely priceless. What did you want to go and offer him our animals for? I thought you said you didn't want to trade them? Have you thought any of this out, and if so, would you mind filling Rudy and me in on your Grand Plan?'

'Calm down, Charlie. I haven't got a plan as such, but we'll figure something out, don't worry.'

'I got Knife,' Rudy advised them, solemnly patting his pocket. Alice winked at him.

'Yes, but let's hope we won't need to use it, Rudy.'

'Anyway, who's Rachel?' Charlie mumbled.

'Don't you get it? She's Old Jim's daughter,' whispered Alice.

Rachel picked up the smaller of the two giant pandas from its playpen and cuddled him in her arms.

'Papa just had them sent from a zoo that was closing down in 2028. He gets a lot of the animals from the time during World War III, because most zoos around the world were having to close then. Some of the animals arrive in very bad condition, but these two came from Edinburgh Zoo and were well cared for.' She put the panda down and he crawled back to his mate, who was munching bamboo.

'We must go now. Dr Foster doesn't like anyone to be late for dinner,' said Rachel, looking at her watch. Alice noticed for the first time that the whites of Rachel's eyes were yellow, like Rudy's. They followed her back into the main part of the villa, up a flight of steps and into the Great Hall, where a long table had been lavishly laid. A maid was lighting some kind of crystal candelabra in the middle of the table, while two others carried in bowls overflowing with tropical fruit.

'Good evening, everyone. I trust you are well rested. Rachel tells me you have met our newest recruits,' said a beaming Dr Foster as he showed them each to their seats. As he came to help Rudy to his place at the table, he said consolingly, 'I can tell by your eyes that you too have suffered from malaria like Rachel. I am sorry you had to endure the mosquitoes on your journey here today. They are a mutant strain that escaped from the biome. It is my fault entirely. A careless lapse in our containment protocols. However, I trust you all found some relief from your stings. The medicine we serve in our jasmine tea will prevent any malaria from developing. It's one of my most lucrative product lines.'

Alice gulped. Had they been exposed to the swarm on purpose? What had they been drugged with? She suddenly felt a little uneasy.

A gong sounded six times.

'Now, where is James? We need to eat.'

But James failed to appear. Dr Foster looked very displeased and growled at a maid, who was dispatched to look for him. The meal proceeded in silence without him. Course after course of strange, exotic food, elaborately piled on enormous platters, were set before them, and Alice noticed that both she and Charlie were struggling to eat any of it. She longed for something simple like the spaghetti with tomato sauce her Dad cooked. Rudy, meanwhile, was noisily tucking into everything, including some craggy-looking things that Dr Foster said were oysters. Alice watched as Rudy hacked one open and slurped the contents into his mouth, just like she'd watched him eat the bird's egg on St Kilda. But the taste of the oyster was obviously not to Rudy's liking, because he immediately spat it out and pushed his plate away, wiping a trail of saliva from his mouth with the back of his hand. The plate caught the edge of the crystal candelabra, which shattered into hundreds of pieces, showering sparkling smithereens all over the table. The maids rushed in to clear up the mess and Alice started apologising and trying to help, when she suddenly realised that Rudy was having some kind of fit. His eyes were rolling and his body was jerking violently.

Dr Foster got up from the table and calmly walked over to a chest of drawers in the corner. He took out a syringe, filled it with a green liquid and proceeded to inject Rudy in the leg. Rudy slumped forward in his chair and passed out.

Alice and Charlie stared in horror, not sure what to say or do, but Dr Foster just snapped his fingers and two maids reappeared with a huge silver tureen.

'And now, the crowning glory of tonight's feast – bird's nest soup!'

Alice shot Charlie a look, remembering the expression on Sam J's face when Charlie had pointed out a bird's nest for sale in the Hong Kong night market for $5,000. Rudy was starting to come round. He looked worse than the morning after he'd drunk Lady Grange's whisky.

Just as they were eating a dessert of stewed grey lychees, which to Alice looked like eyeballs and tasted of perfume, James walked into the room. He was older than she remembered, with grey strands in amongst his brown hair and beard, and he now walked with a limp. But he still had the same speedy determination.

'Foster, I demand an answer right now or this whole project is over!' he bellowed as he strode right up to his business partner. Rudy jumped and almost fell off his chair.

'Not now, James. Can't you see we have company?' Dr Foster replied sweetly, his hand gesturing in a circular flourish to indicate the others round the table.

James sighed and ran his hands through his hair. He seemed to have something very troubling on his mind as he sat down heavily in the last remaining chair at the table, opposite Alice, with his head in his hands. Alice wanted to attract his attention, but he was so preoccupied that he hadn't even noticed who his guests were. She stretched out her leg under the table and kicked him on the shin. James looked up with a start and stared at her.

There was a very odd moment when their eyes met, and Alice saw the flicker of recognition pass across James' face. His lips moved briefly, as if he was mouthing her name, and then he shot a quick sideways glance at Dr Foster. There was no doubt in Alice's mind that he knew exactly who she was, but it was also obvious that, in the present circumstances, he could not afford to let his business partner see that he knew her.

From that moment, James' mood seemed to change dramatically. He turned to his business partner and said politely, 'Dr Foster, aren't you going to introduce me to everyone?'

'My dear James, of course,' said Foster, faltering slightly. 'But forgive me, my memory is very poor these days. Would you good people mind introducing yourselves to James and say why you are here? You see, James, they have some new animals to offer us.'

Chapter 17: Nightflight

Alice was back in their quarters and almost asleep when she heard the paper screen slide back and in the semi-darkness she could see a man creep into their room. He moved quickly between Charlie and Rudy's sleeping bodies as if he was looking for something or someone. She half closed her eyes and pretended to be asleep when suddenly he tapped her on the shoulder.

'What on earth are you doing here Alice?' he hissed, 'I nearly had a heart attack when I realized it was you at dinner!'

It was James.

'We came to stop Dr Foster going ahead with Plan B,' she whispered.

'However do you know about Plan B? It's classified information.'

Alice didn't know what to say without breaking her own time traveller rules, so she remained silent.

'Never mind, the thing is, now that you're here, it occurs to me you could help me out. I take it you arrived in the C-Bean Mark 3?'

'Mark 4, actually,' Alice confirmed. She had no idea where the conversation was leading.

'I see. Listen, can we go somewhere a bit more private. I don't want to others to hear what I've got to tell you.'

Alice slid out of bed and slipped on her silk slippers. They padded silently out of the room and sat in the courtyard beside the water sculpture, in what Alice thought was a patch of moonlight, until she realized it was an artificial moon mounted on the glass roof of the biome.

'I need a way out. Foster has become impossible to work with. I don't know how much you know about it, but he's started exploiting our Operation Seabean project in ways I could never have imagined, to the extent he's now talking about making money on the side from smuggling people back in time. Last month I had to stop him from sending a secret pilot consignment of twenty people from Hong Kong back to 2027, but the list of names got out. Øbsidon's been constantly in the news ever since and vigilante gangs have sprung up all over the DZ. Like you, they're hell bent on stopping Plan B from going ahead, But Foster doesn't seem to care – he just calls it 'bad publicity' and says it doesn't matter as long as no one knows where Øbsidon's HQ is. His mind is set. He wants to 'assist' all the people who are basically unhappy with their lot in 2077 and want out. It was bad enough when he started to produce and sell infertile clones of all the plant and animal species I was importing from the past. But now this … As far as I'm concerned it's all gone far enough. And to top it all, his latest plans for developing the C-Bean further involve using a very unstable isotope of Øbsidon – something I can't possibly agree to.'

'So what are you going to do?' Alice asked, curious.

'I hadn't got the foggiest idea until you turned up this evening, Alice. Once again, your timing is impeccable! I desperately need to borrow your C-Bean to get away from here – back to my own time – and take Rachel with me. I should have done it when she was a baby after her mother died, but I couldn't be sure the C-Bean Mark 1 that I built to Foster's design was safe enough to go backwards through time, and we are still having development issues with the Mark 2. From the maths I've done, it looks as if there could be some pretty nasty genetic side effects.'

Alice wondered if he meant that peculiar feeling of being rearranged that she'd noticed when they first travelled in the C-Bean Mark 4.

'So I've developed a chemical antidote – Foster doesn't know I've been working on it – so far I've manufactured only a very small amount of it – about half a dozen doses, using, would you believe it, three parts durian juice mixed with one part artificial gold and some other ingredients. I'd made enough for Rachel and me to be protected from the side effects of going back in the C-Bean Mark 2 – but now you're here too, we'll have to split it. I hope there's enough. How many of you in total have gone backwards in time so far?'

Alice stopped to think.

'Four, I think. The others have only gone forwards in time up til now. But if you mean how many of us need to get back to 2018, it's 8 in total. Oh, and Lori. So nine.'

James frowned and tugged his beard for a moment.

'Who's Lori?'

'My sister.'

'Is everyone more or less the same weight as you?'

'Yes, except Rudy, he's the heaviest.'

'Should be fine then – I have six adult doses but more if I split them into kids' doses. Now, where exactly did you leave the C-Bean?'

'On the roof of Charlie's granddad's old apartment building back in Hong Kong. Are you serious about this James? The Mark 4 does makes you feel a bit weird – even Charlie and I have noticed that.'

'It's a risk we'll have to take. There isn't any alternative! Here's the plan: you go back in there and wake the others. I will get Rachel and pack our things. I'll book a personal Maglev to take us back to Hong Kong quickly tonight, before Foster realizes what's going on.'

'Personal Maglev?'

'Magnetic Levitator. It's a sort of high speed taxi that works by magnetism – they laid the guideway track over the lagoon in the 2040s – it's old hat now, but still, a great invention, just a shame it can't teleport through time too!'

'OK, but I can't leave without our pets Spex and Spix – Dr Foster took them both away from us before dinner. He said he would offer us a price in the morning. But I don't really want to sell them to him at all – it was the only way we could get inside the biome without causing suspicion.'

'Rachel will know where they are, come on, there's not much time. Meet you back here in twenty minutes.' And with that, James disappeared through a door in the corner of the courtyard.

Rachel arrived with two animal carry cages when they returned. Her face was white with nerves and Alice could tell she had no idea why they were all stealing away from the biome, from her home, in the dead of night.

'Here you are, Alice,' she said, 'I wanted to bring the pandas too, but Papa said I couldn't. I don't know why.' A tear rolled down Rachel's face.

'I'm sorry, Rachel darling, but it's for the best,' James said consolingly, 'Now everyone, this way, quickly.'

James led them out through a back entrance to the waiting Maglev, which turned out to be a long, sleek, silver, bullet-shaped pod. He loaded two large bags into the back of the hovering vehicle, and when all five of them plus the two animals were safely inside, the Maglev sped off, skimming rapidly above the surface of the vast inland lagoon back to Hong Kong.

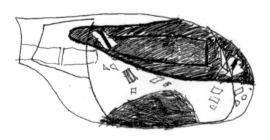

James unzipped one of the bags and pulled out a neat insulated case. When he opened it, Alice saw it was lined with rows of compartments, most of them containing a small phial of liquid. Tucked into a pocket in the side of the case was another of his leather notebooks. When they were a safe distance from the biome he spoke.

'These are the time travel antidote doses, Alice.' James checked the labels on each of the phials, and then showed her the notebook.

'I'm giving you this too. Everything is in here – all the work I've been doing at Øbsidon, the whole of Plan B, including the formula for Øbsidon itself. It's all in my head too, of course. Thanks to you arriving when you did, we're already more than halfway to stopping Foster from going any further with Plan B. I managed to wipe all our research files from the computer servers before I left the biome as well as taking my share of the gold from the vault, so with any luck Foster and his minions wont be able to continue with his evil project because he will have neither the computer code nor the investment funds to proceed. He'll have to stick to developing the habitat like we discussed. The world in 2077 needs to restore biodiversity, so there's nothing wrong with Plan A as a legitimate and constructive use of time travel, but as for all this human trafficking racket, I want nothing to do with it. I think I've dealt with everything. Now, let's find your C-Bean and get back to 1977.'

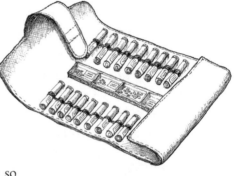

They arrived at the base of Harbourside Tower 6 just as it was getting light. Alice and Charlie each took a carry cage, leaving Rudy and James to carry the bags up thirty-two flights of stairs. Half way up they heard noises on one of the landings and James muttered something about it most likely being a gang of vigilantes.

'We waiting for you,' the gang leader announced in a gruff voice when they reached the next floor. He stood barring their way on the broken concrete landing, an immense bare-chested Chinese guy covered with elaborate tattoos and multiple scars. 'Girl here tell us you coming back,' he added, dragging someone from behind him. She was gagged and blindfolded and wearing a black hoodie. Alice suddenly realized it was Karla.

James spoke back to him in Cantonese and took the gang leader by surprise, which gave Rudy enough time to flick open his penknife. He lunged towards the gang leader, while James swung a bag at two of the others, clipping them on the head and knocking them out cold against the stair balustrade. It gave Rachel enough time to slip past them and up another flight, but the gang leader had by then produced a handgun from the holster and was pressing to Rudy's head, taunting him in a loud voice.

'Come on, Mr Yellow Eyes. Better tell us where Øbsidon is or I shoot girl!'

Alice could see Rudy was getting angry and upset. He twisted round and grabbed the gang leader's wrist to free Karla from his grip. They both edged closer to a gap in the stair balustrade.

'You making me angry, Yellow Eyes!' the gang leader muttered ominously.

The gang leader cocked the trigger on his gun in readiness to shoot. Another gang member was creeping closer. Rudy managed to kick him sideways and the man stumbled. Karla stood in their midst, shaking with fear. Her head hung down and her hands were tied behind her with a dirty rag. Rudy lunged towards the end of the rag and tugged it loose but just at that moment the gang leader pulled the trigger and shot Rudy in the arm.

Alice gasped. She realized Karla couldn't see what was happening.

'Karla move away!' she blurted out.

Karla's head lifted slightly as if she'd just realized Alice was there. She shuffled back a step or two.

'No Karla, the other way!' Alice yelled as Karla lost her footing on the broken edge of a step. She lost her footing and fell between the gap in the balustrade, plummeting down the stairwell. James jumped forward and reached out to try and grab her, but it was too late. There was a thud as her body landed on the marble floor fifteen stories below.

Alice shrieked and Rudy peered over the edge of the landing.

'She dead!' he growled, angrily turning on the gang leader with raised fists. There was a scuffle as he tried to wrestle the gang leader to the ground.

'Rudy, be careful!' yelled Alice.

She looked up the stairwell and saw that Charlie had blocked the way using with the two animal cages to protect Rachel, who was crying on the landing above them. Both animals had somehow escaped from their cages. Spix was flying frantically around in the stairwell squawking 'Muito Mau, Muito Mau,' while Spex rushed up and down the broken steps barking. Suddenly James threw an emergency flare into their midst. A massive cloud of red smoke billowed around them, making it impossible for anyone to see each other. Someone let off a round of bullets and the gang members dispersed, shouting to one another in Cantonese. Alice heard one say the word 'police' and from the echoing voices it sounded like they ran off into an empty apartment.

Her eyes streaming with tears and smoke, Alice managed to find the handrail and started climbing the stairs. Charlie was calling down to her and she could hear James' footsteps up ahead, but she couldn't see a thing. Eventually they emerged on the roof, coughing and spluttering in the morning air, including Spix and Spex. As Alice regained her sight, the first thing she noticed was that the gang had obviously discovered the C-Bean, because across its black surface in graffiti were the words '∅BSIDON: BURN IN HELL!'. She commanded the door to open and everyone stepped into the C-Bean. Everyone, that is, except Rudy.

Alice's Blog #6

Friday 21st September 2018

I can't stop thinking about what happened in Hong Kong. It was bad enough what happened to Karla, but then it got even worse. After we'd escaped back to the C-Bean on the roof, we huddled together inside until we were sure the coast was clear. James and I left Rachel with Charlie and went with Spex to look for Rudy.

We found him lying face down on the landing. James turned him over. Blood was seeping out of his side and his yellow eyes were rolling. We tried to pick him up, but he groaned with pain. Spex ran round in circles whining in sympathy. James gave him something to ease the pain. All I could do was hold Rudy's hand. He made me cry when he said to me 'It OK Alice. Going to see family. Little sister, Mama, Papa, all together now.' Then he took the severed finger out of his pocket and gave it to me, like it was a precious gift. He smiled and said 'Might need Deadman Finger'.

Torches started flashing from the lobby below and just as James whispered it was the military police, Rudy started having a seizure. There was this horrific moment when his body just seemed to go limp. James checked his heart to find it wasn't beating any more and told me Rudy was dead. My own heart almost stopped beating too when I heard that. James had to carry me back to the C-Bean. As he lay me down on the floor, I realized I was covered in blood.

I asked him 'Am I bleeding, James?'

'No, it's Rudy's,' he told me grimly. 'Now let's just take the antidote and go home.' I have no idea how we managed to get Rachel and James back to 1977, but Charlie tells me we managed somehow and then got ourselves home.

You can imagine the scene when we arrived back on St Kilda in 2018: Our parents were beside themselves – although they were overjoyed that Charlie and I had reappeared, it was two whole days since we'd vanished and we were in a terrible state – dehydrated, dirty, wearing some strange oriental clothing, and covered in someone else's blood. And on top of that, none of what we said made any sense to them. I was crying about someone called Rudy, and Charlie was trying to explain to them that Rudy had kidnapped Karla Ingermann but that she'd died in an unfortunate accident. As far as they were concerned, we'd both gone missing the day the marine biologists arrived, and the last person to see us was Edie. She'd told them we must have done something stupid, but she didn't know what. I could kill her for saying that. At least she didn't mention anything about the C-Bean.

Needless to say, I am not allowed out of the house now. Charlie is grounded too. This morning he texted me 'Sorry about Spex'. It's been so bad I hadn't even noticed he didn't come back with us – apparently the poor dog wouldn't leave Rudy's side when he died, so James had to leave him there. Now Spix won't leave my side. He keeps saying over and over in a demented high-pitched sing-song 'Spix-Spex Spix-Spex'. It's driving me mad but I can't make him stop. Mum says someone is coming over from the Outer Hebrides mental health team to talk to me on Monday. But there's nothing they can do to help. Unless they can explain to me why it's always got to be like this! I mean, why it is that every time we manage to make something good happen, something terrible has to happen as well.

Monday 24th September 2018

Edie came to see me after school today. She apologised for getting us into trouble. I was a bit grumpy towards her at first, but eventually I told her everything that happened to Charlie and me, and now she feels really bad that she didn't come with us.

I'm supposed to be going back to school tomorrow, but I just don't feel up to it. And I have this awful tummy ache all the time; it feels like when you get a stitch. Mum says that she can't let me go on the trip to our new school in Glasgow unless I show some signs of improvement soon and I do really want to go, so I guess I'll have to force myself to show up at school. Charlie went back to school last Friday, even though he says he's got stomachache too. It's my heart that hurts more. It's so hard feeling sad about losing two people that no one here even knows, and worse than that, that they think you're making it all up.

Friday 28th September 2018

School was actually quite fun this week. I'm going to make a real effort from now on with my schoolwork, because I've realized it's the best way to get over everything that's happened. There are lots of things to look forward to – like the Armistice Day Centenary Celebrations on November 11th – apparently some of the people whose families used to live here and whose relatives from St Kilda served in the war are coming over that day to mark the occasion. Mum has got us all working on a project about the First World War and why it happened and how they managed to end it on Armistice Day. I can't help wondering about World War III and how that will start and what will make it end. I don't think war achieves anything. It just seems to mess everything up and make things worse. I said in class today that it would be far better if instead of going to war, we could think of a way to stop the sea from rising and all the animals from becoming extinct. But Mum just said it was 'besides the point' and that we would be doing a project about climate change and the environment next term. Why don't adults realize they are all connected? It's like they're pretending it's not really happening because it's just too difficult to deal with.

Monday 1st October 2018, St Kilda

Mum says she's booked for Edie and me to go by ferry to the mainland on Friday morning. When we get there, we have to get the train by ourselves from Oban to Glasgow, and someone from Lori's school will be there to meet us. Edie's really nervous but I can't wait.

Friday 5th October 2018, Glasgow

We arrived at 7 o'clock this evening. There are girls here from twenty-two other schools around Scotland. I sat next to a few of them at dinner and they seem nice but a bit talkative – they've all seen the latest films and know lots more about pop music than Edie and me. Some of the girls had been to some really exotic places on holiday this summer like Turkey, Disneyland and the Maldives. When it was our turn to introduce ourselves, I really wanted to say that I'd been all over the world, that I'd been to London once in 1851, that I'd visited a real rainforest in 2118, and that I'd cuddled pandas in Hong Kong in 2077, but of course I couldn't, so I just said 'My name is Alice, I come from St Kilda, the furthest-away islands in Scotland, and I have a pet parrot called Spix'.

After dinner, we were allowed to buy sweets in the tuck shop and then we were taken back to our dorms. I saw Lori in the corridor, but she more or less ignored me. I was probably wearing something she didn't approve of. The other girls all arrived in school uniform but as we don't have uniform at our school, I wanted to wear jeans and my flowery wellies like I usually do, but Mum said we needed to look a bit smart, so I ended up wearing my stripy rainbow fleece with a boring brown skirt, socks and trainers.

I'm sharing a room with Edie and this other girl called Lucy. She's from Edinburgh. I asked her if there were pandas at Edinburgh Zoo these days. I was going to ask her something else but Edie gave me this look that said 'don't say anything weird or I'll kill you', so I changed the subject.

The really cool thing is, we are having an English lesson tomorrow and it's going to be about *The Time Machine* by H.G.Wells – the teachers gave us each a very scruffy copy of the book after dinner and said we had to read up to chapter three before tomorrow morning. I wish Donald was here too – that's his favourite book!

Saturday 6th October 2018, Glasgow

It feels funny being at school at a weekend. Instead of wandering down to the beach after breakfast with Spex like I often do on a Saturday, I had to sit in a massive classroom and answer mental maths questions. After that the English teacher took us for a lesson. She got us to read bits of *The Time Machine* out loud in turn. My bit had this sentence:

'I am afraid I cannot convey the peculiar sensations of time travelling, they are excessively unpleasant.'

It made me wonder if the author had been inside a C-Bean Mark 4. The teacher talked about other writers who have written books about time travel and then she told us we had to write a short story about what we thought it would feel like. I thought to myself, that shouldn't be too hard! But the thing is, I didn't have enough time to finish my story because there was so much to say. The teacher picked me to read mine out because she'd noticed I'd written quite a lot, and the other girls all stared when I started describing the Dead Zone, the Biome, and especially all the stuff about how the C-Bean works. Edie went bright red when I was reading, probably because she was petrified I was going to bring her into the story at any moment.

After lunch we had some free time and some of the prefects took us into the centre of Glasgow on the bus. Edie and I were put in Lori's group, which I wasn't too keen on, mainly because she acts so weird when her friends are there. But she did let us do some fun things, like have a milkshake in an Italian café a bit like the one we went to in New York with Dr Foster. She also let us look round a funny little curio shop that was all dark inside and sold a lot of musty old things like stuffed birds and animals in glass domes, collections of coins and medals and bits of rock.

Lori whispered in my ear 'See that creepy guy over there – that's who bought the gold nugget Alice.' I got a bit of a shock when I realized the person she was talking about looked exactly like Dr Foster. Seeing his face brought back the sharp pains in my stomach, but I managed to duck behind a bookcase before he saw me. It was probably another of Hadron's cyborgs, but unless I got up close enough to see if he was wearing an identity bracelet, I couldn't be sure. Then it suddenly occurred to me it could be the real Dr Foster and that he'd come looking for James, not realizing he died in July. All I knew was that I had to get out of the shop.

Chapter 18: Contaminated

Alice and Edie were getting ready for bed in their dormitory. Their roommate Lucy was in the bathroom and Alice sat on her bed holding her toothbrush and towel, waiting her turn. Her stomachache had got a lot worse.

'It's been quite fun, but I'll be glad to get back to St Kilda,' Edie said as she folded her clothes and put them in her suitcase.

'Me too. I don't know what I've eaten today but I feel really ill,' Alice admitted.

By the time the prefects came round to tell them it was lights out, Alice was doubled up in agony on the bathroom floor. Someone went to fetch Lori, who stood over her sister with her hands on her hips, saying 'Come on Alice, pull yourself together.'

But Alice just writhed with pain. In the end, they called the night Warden and she sent for an ambulance.

Lori and Mrs Blythe, the Warden went with her to the hospital, and while Alice was being admitted to the children's ward Lori used Mrs Blythe's mobile phone to call her parents.

As soon as a doctor examined her, Alice was taken into the operating theatre. One of the nurses told Lori to wait outside and that her sister was being treated for suspected appendicitis. Lori frowned and wondered if she should say anything to Mrs Blythe. Something didn't add up: her parents said on the phone that Charlie was also ill, doubled up with stomach pain, and when they asked Lori to describe Alice's symptoms, they decided to tell the Cheungs to call for an air ambulance to send Charlie to Glasgow Hospital too. Her parents had said Charlie and Alice had both been up to something, something to do with that C-Bean again. Whatever it was, Lori knew there was no way they could both have simultaneously developed appendicitis. It just didn't seem possible.

When Alice came round, she found herself lying in a hospital bed surrounded by her parents, her sister and her baby brother and Charlie was in the next bed with his parents.

'What's going on?' she asked restlessly.

'Just relax, darling. We're right here – Dad and I are staying overnight with Kit in a hotel near the hospital. The doctors say it's not appendicitis after all, but they're working hard to try to work out what's the matter with you both,' Alice's mother replied, her face drawn and pale.

'They found traces of something unusual in your blood, Alice. They wanted to know if you'd been travelling somewhere exotic recently,' whispered her father, adding in an even quieter voice, 'whatever it is, Charlie's blood tests showed up the same thing. You also both have something very strange on your arms, some kind of metal insert. Is there something you haven't told us Alice?'

Alice sighed wearily, lay back on her pillow and closed her eyes. She thought of all the exotic places they'd been to recently that her parents had no idea about and all the things they'd eaten and drunk: the weird banquet at Øbsidon HQ in Hong Kong in 2077, not to mention the disgusting food rations, dirty tap water and soup they'd had on St Kilda in 2118. Any one of them could have given them some deadly virus, and judging by the weather they'd encountered in the future, even the air they'd breathed could have caused their mystery illness. They could easily have been infected by the water in the Dead Zone, or when their bioports were fitted, or poisoned by the swarm of mutant mosquitoes or, for that matter, by the drug Dr Foster had put in their tea to stop them getting malaria. Then Alice remembered James' antidote to combat the effects of travelling back in time. Could it have been that? But before she could even begin to answer her own questions, Alice fell asleep.

She seemed to be drifting along an endless corridor. All the doors had windows and were labeled with different dates and there were people inside each room. She peered through the windows one by one as she went past and saw Lady Grange reunited with her family, Dora Ferguson with Donald, Elsa and baby James in her arms, Karla as a little red-haired girl playing a game with Kit, and Rudy with his mother and father and little sister sitting round a table eating bowls of rice. She tried to get inside the rooms but the doors were all locked. In the last room she saw a family gathered round a hospital bed. When she turned the handle, she found this door was not locked and she went inside the room. The little boy and his older sister turned to see who it was as she entered. She opened her mouth to speak but no words came out. 'Come and say goodbye to Mum, Alice,' Lori said to her and the boy pulled her towards the figure lying in the bed. 'Is that Alice, Kit? Is she here now?' The mother said softly. The little boy nodded. 'Have you got a seabean to give to Alice too?' he asked.

Someone was gripping Alice's arm. She opened her eyes. It was dark in the ward and he was standing over her, his face sweaty and his body shaking. At first she thought she was the mother lying in the hospital bed. She was sure she was in a hospital. But the boy leaning over her was not Kit. It was Charlie.

'Alice, listen, I've looked at our notes – you know the clipboard at the end of our beds – it says we've got acute blood poisoning from unknown contaminants. It doesn't look good. We have to do something tonight or I think we're going to die!' his voice sounded strange and high-pitched.

'Charlie, relax, the doctors are doing what they can, my parents said so,' Alice assured him, but she could feel a rising tide of panic inside her as the pain in her stomach started to return. The dream had disturbed her and the painkillers she'd been given at bedtime must have worn off.

'Look, I brought the C-Bean's cardkey with me just in case. I think we should use it. If we go back in time to the day before we time-travelled to Liverpool in the C-Bean, whatever it was that's made us ill won't have happened.'

'Nor will a lot of other important things, Charlie. Let's not react too quickly. I need to think about this.' She paused. They were both breathing a short, shallow gasps.

Alice cast her mind back to the start of term, the day they got back to St Kilda and she'd decided to make the time capsule. It was, she realized with a shock, only six weeks ago. So much had happened since then. It seemed so ironic that they had been the ones who found the time capsule a hundred years later, not some archaeologist like Charlie thought. If Donald had left a time capsule in the same cave under the gun a hundred years ago back in 1918, Alice realized they might have found that one too in 2018 when the Sams discovered the cave. Even Lady Grange herself was a sort of time capsule, imprisoned on the island in the eighteenth century until Alice found her and brought her back to 2018. Looking back, the first aid kit they'd left on St Kilda for the dying babies and the food hamper for the starving villagers in 1851 were a kind of reverse time capsule, left in the past by people from the future, to help solve their problems or the unforeseen outcomes they were causing.

But how could they go back in time and solve their own problems? What should they leave in the past to help things turn out right? If, as Charlie suggested, they used the C-Bean to go back to a time before the sleepover, they would avoid being abducted to 2118. Better still, if they used the C-Bean to go back to the morning of Alice's birthday in January, when the black cube first arrived on the beach, and then just ignored it altogether, they wouldn't get into any of the difficulties they'd experienced.

But Alice had this nagging feeling in the back of her mind. The very thought of rewinding events like that made her realize the experiences she'd had because of the C-Bean were more important to her than anything else. Even the really awful tragic things they'd had to deal with because of meeting Karla, Donald, James, Dr Foster and Rudy, were part of her own life now.

'Remember what you said to me the night Karla told us that Kit was her dad, Charlie?'

'What did I say?'

'You said we should use what we know about the future to make things less bad.'

'Sort of, why?'

'Well I'm ready to do something about it now,' Alice said slowly.

'Good. Let's go back to St Kilda the day we were due to leave for Liverpool, and actually go on the ferry this time.'

'That's the thing, Charlie. I'm not ready to wipe everything that's happened from our existence – I mean from our memories – by going right back to before any of it happened. That would make us cowards.'

'OK. So what *do* we do?' Charlie demanded.

'Let's at least try to pinpoint what's made us sick. If Edie and Hannah are OK it can't have been something we were exposed to in Brazil, or when we were imprisoned in the C-Bean in Hadron's compound. So it must have been after that.'

'Reckon it was the dodgy tap water? Or that packet of soup mix you cooked? Our bioports?'

'Edie has one too, remember?'

'What about James' antidote – do you think it could have been that?'

'The antidote … you've just given me an idea, Charlie.'

Lost in thought, Alice climbed out of bed and stood up, panting and grimacing with pain. Her legs felt weak and jelly-like, but her mind was made up.

'Charlie, where's the C-Bean's cardkey? I know the answer.'

The two children crept out of the ward and into the day room at the end, where they pulled the curtains across so that no one could see them from the nurse's station. Alice shoved a couple of armchairs out of the way, to clear a space in the middle of the room that was big enough for the C-Bean to fit into. It left her feeling dizzier and more wobbly than ever. She sat down on the one of the chairs to get her breath back before summoning the black cube, and when it appeared it only just fitted – the top of it was practically touching the suspended ceiling. They stepped inside, once again wearing their pyjamas, and Charlie looked quizzically at Alice.

'OK, so what's the plan?' he asked.

'Remember in May when Karla and I did a factory reset on the C-Bean and we accidentally went back to 1918?'

'Yep.'

'Well, I don't think I ever told you but we went on a little school trip with Dora and Donald to the Great Exhibition in 1851.'

'You did what?'

'It was Donald's idea – he just wanted to time travel somewhere for real and that's what they'd just been learning about in history.'

'And?'

'We arrived in this massive glass building in the middle of Hyde Park in London. I remember wondering what the Victorians would make of our futuristic C-Bean, but I used the invisible command for the first time, so until it started wearing off, no one could actually see it.'

'Alice, can you please get to the point – we haven't got time for a long-winded story!'

'Ok, be patient, I'm getting to it. What if we go back there now, but this time with a whole bunch of things that are visible? Whatever we take with us, the Victorians will assume they're amazing modern inventions from somewhere or other – the whole place was full of them. But in actual fact, our C-Bean would be a sort of time capsule, delivering on a plate to people in 1851 all the knowhow from the future that would mean they never have to burn fossil fuels to make their factories and their vehicles run, because they would have the technology to get all the energy they need from the wind or the waves or the sun. Think about it, Charlie – it'd be the best antidote ever!' Alice's face was flushed with excitement.

'Maybe your parents are right after all – you have gone bonkers!'

'I'm not bonkers Charlie. This is the way we can use what we know about the future, just like you said. This is how we can change everything. If we give the Victorians enough information – show them what our dads already know – that it's cheaper and cleaner to use things like wave power instead of burning coal and oil – the ice won't melt, the sea won't rise, the animals won't die, get the picture? There'll be no need for either Plan A or Plan B – that'll mean no need for Operation Seabean whatsoever!'

Alice paused for breath, her eyes shining.

'I suppose it could work,' Charlie admitted.

'It *will* work – all the damage to the earth's atmosphere was done after 1851, Dad told me. You never know, it might even prevent wars from happening.'

Charlie sighed and slumped onto the floor.

'But what can the two of us do in the state we're in?'

'You're right, we need help. Let me think ...'

Alice appeared to be lost in thought. But the C-Bean produced a map showing the layout of the Great Exhibition indicating a suitable space to set up their exhibit in 1851 without obstructing the red carpet walkway. It said the whole exhibition was due to close on the 11th October, but one or two of the Russian exhibitors had already vacated their spaces, so it chose one of their empty stands. Then it produced detailed 3D scale models of the latest solar panels, wave energy machines and wind turbines in large recesses around its walls. Alice clapped her hands with delight at these miniature worlds: there was a wind farm installed on a mountainside, a hydro-electric plant like a mini Niagara falls, a solar energy farm in a desert, and of course, a model of the Evaw wave energy device their own fathers had built in the sea west of St Kilda. Before long they could hardly move in the C-Bean because it was so full of exhibits. Alice looked at her watch – it was four o'clock in the morning. She was aching all over with the effort of it all and her stomach ache felt like a knife slicing through her.

'Nice work, Alice, but how ever are we going to get all of this stuff to London? I'm really not feeling great.'

'Me neither, Charlie,' Alice said weakly.

'Maybe we should just call it quits.'

'Wait, I know who could help us: Kit.'

'What? Where on earth are we going to find him? There's no way I'm going back to Øbsidon.'

'We don't have to go there. He's right here in this hospital by my mother's bedside, in 2029.'

The C-Bean didn't seem to need any further instruction. The models all shunted slightly from side to side and then came to a standstill. They appeared to have timeshifted.

'Wait here, Charlie, I'll be back.'

Alice stepped out of the C-Bean into the day room. She peeped round the curtain and saw the children's ward was still in darkness. As she passed her bed, she could see there was another child asleep there. So far, so good. The nurses' station was in a different place and there were no staff working there except for a strange white robot filing paperwork. She managed to avoid attracting the robot's attention and slipped out of the ward into the main corridor. A little unsteady on her feet, Alice walked back to the reception desk and asked the night porter if he could look something up on the computer system for her.

The night porter scratched his head, peered at Alice and frowned.

'What are you doing down here young lady? It's the middle of the night.'

'I know, but I sleepwalk and now I can't remember where my bed or my ward is. Please help me – my name's Jennifer Robertson.'

He chuckled to himself and tapped in the name on his keyboard.

'Ward 16, first floor, bed nine. Down the corridor, take the lift up one floor, turn right.'

'By the way, what's tomorrow's date?'

'6th October 2029, now off you go.'

'Thank you,' Alice called, hurrying back along the main corridor.

When she reached Ward 16, there was a row of seats outside the double doors. Her stomachache was really starting to trouble her now, and she sat down to rest for a moment in one of the seats. Just as she was about to gather her strength and enter the ward to look for her family, the double doors swung open and a boy with red hair and freckles came out.

'Kit?'

The boy glanced in her direction with a sorrowful expression on his face. He was clutching something in his hand.

'Who are you?'

'May I see the seabean?

The boy looked surprised, and opened his palm to reveal a shiny round seed.

'Did your Mum just give it to you?'

He nodded, welling up.

'She's very sick isn't she?'

He nodded again.

'What would you say if I told you I know a way to help her survive?'

'It's too late, the doctors said.'

'Kit, it's not too late, come with me,' Alice urged, taking his hand. He was exactly the same size as her.

'But Lori told me to wait here.'

'It won't take long, I promise. But I need your help.'

'OK.'

And with that, the two eleven-year-old children walked in silence back to the ward where Alice had left the C-Bean.

Alice's Blog #7

7th October 2018

When we got back to the day room, I told Kit to stand in front of the curtain. But before I pulled it aside, he turned to me with a very solemn look on his freckly face and whispered 'You came in the C-Bean, didn't you? Is that what's behind the curtain Alice?' I was completely dumbstruck. Kit had somehow worked out who I was and how I'd got there.

'You don't have to explain, Alice. You used to tell me stories about the C-Bean all the time when I was little. You told me I had to keep them a secret because no one else knew about it. Mum just used to laugh and said you had a very vivid imagination, but I knew somehow it was all true. I just never thought I'd get to see it with my own eyes,' he said simply.

I pulled back the curtain then, and Kit walked round and round the C-Bean, just like I did when I first found it on the beach. He left a trail of little blue handprints all over the black exterior until finally he found the door.

'Make it open, Alice,' he whispered, holding his breath.

Moments later me, my brother and my best friend, stepped out of the C-Bean into the Great Exhibition in Hyde Park. As soon as I caught sight of the huge glass roof and the elm trees, I knew we were in the right place, even though it was the middle of the night and the whole place was completely deserted.

I asked the C-Bean for three torches but it went one better and produced the kind of torches you wear on your head like a miner. We pulled the stretchy bands around our heads and adjusted the beam of light so that they shone out in front of us. Then we started to carry or drag all the exhibits out of the C-Bean and arrange them on the empty stand left by the Russians. I found a ladder leaning against one of the iron columns and Kit climbed up, took down their old sign and put ours up instead. It read:

'ENERGY OF THE FUTURE:
COME AND SEE HOW WIND, SUN, WAVES AND WATER
CAN PROVIDE ALL THE POWER WE WILL EVER NEED'

It didn't take Kit long to realize that Charlie and I were very ill. He ended up doing most of the work, poor boy, lugging the models into place. Once everything was arranged just how I'd imagined it, the C-Bean seemed to take over and add some finishing touches of its own. We all watched in amazement as a vivid stream of holograms started to flow out of the C-Bean and, one by one, brought all the 3D models to life. I think the C-Bean wanted to make sure the Victorian visitors understood exactly how each invention worked. It transformed our modest exhibition with real clouds, rainstorms, waterfalls and ocean waves. There was even a miniature sun above it all casting warm golden rays on the models below. It was definitely the C-Bean's finest moment!

The effort of producing these special effects seemed to have exhausted the C-Bean too, because its outer surface started pulsating with weird patterns, then it started flipping from black to gold and back again. A strange countdown sequence started, and the C-Bean remained golden, shimmering and luminous as if it was lit from within.

That was the moment I panicked, because I remembered the last time it did that – just after we arrived in Liverpool – the C-Bean vanished! I shouted to Kit and Charlie to get back inside but I don't remember anything after that. I must have blacked out.

I still have no idea how my brother managed to control the C-Bean. He must have somehow issued a command to take him back to 2029, and then send Charlie and me to the same hospital but in 2018. Maybe the C-Bean realized he was my brother and that I was too ill to control it myself any more. Anyway, it doesn't matter, I'm just happy that Kit is going to grow up with the memory of what we did that night.

Chapter 20: Gone

When Alice woke she found herself lying in her bed in the dormitory. She sat up quickly and looked over at Edie and Lucy still asleep in the beds next to her. She felt very confused. Why wasn't she still in hospital with Charlie next to her? Had she somehow recovered overnight and been brought back to the school? She was relieved to discover her stomach ache had gone. She rolled up her sleeve. The bioport had gone too. In fact it looked like it had never been there.

Alice had a tiny feeling of dread when she reached under her pillow for the notebook where she'd been drafting her blog entries. It was still there. She sat up in bed, turned on her bedside light and started to flick through the pages. She'd written in it the evening before, but had said nothing about being rushed to hospital, nothing about going back to 1851 in the C-Bean with Kit and Charlie. She turned back a few pages to read the earlier entries, only to find there was no mention of James Ferguson or Rachel and their escape from the biome, and nothing at all about Commander Hadron or Dr Foster. She was even more shocked to find she hadn't said a single thing about Karla or Rudy and their terrible deaths. But most importantly, she seemed to have written nothing whatsoever about the C-Bean. Alice flicked all the way back to the start of the book, which was dated 1st August, expecting to find an account of the house fire and their trip to Liverpool at least, maybe even something about her plans to bury a time capsule. But instead, the notebook contained one long, boring account of everything they'd been doing at school since the start of term. About three pages in she'd commented how she still felt sad about Old Jim passing away in July, and on another about how she longed for a dog. Apart from that, even though she knew it was her own handwriting, Alice could hardly recognize her own life as depicted in the notebook.

It was hard to take it all in. Why was there nothing recorded there about all the hundreds of things she could remember as having happened when the events were all still so vivid in her mind, especially of last night? Could it be that the only thing that hadn't disappeared were her own memories? Alice gulped. This feeling of having your head messed with was worse than the feeling of your insides being rearranged in the C-Bean Mark 4. What if she was the only one that could remember anything now about the C-Bean?

'Morning,' Edie said sleepily from the next bed, 'are you still reading that rubbish Time Machine book Alice?'

'So we did at least do that ...' Alice murmured slowly, turning to look at her friend. 'Edie did I read out a story yesterday in class about a time travel device called a C-Bean?'

'No, why?'

'Nothing.'

Everything was different. Or back to normal, depending how Alice looked at it. Either way, life had taken some getting used to when she returned to St Kilda after her trip to Glasgow. Her parents had commented that she seemed more thoughtful and mature afterwards, and decided the experience had obviously been good for her. But Alice simply had a lot on her mind.

Her parents were still the same people, and she still had a little brother called Kit and a big sister called Lori, there were still six children in her class and her mum was still their teacher. But that's about where the similarities to her other life ended. As far as everyone on the island was concerned, no one, not even Charlie or Edie, had ever heard of something called a C-Bean, they'd never met Lady Grange, Dr Foster or Karla Ingermann, and they couldn't recall there ever being a dog called Spex or a parrot called Spix on St Kilda. Even the reason the Robertsons were living there was different – Alice's dad was in charge of renewable energy across the whole of Scotland, and managed a hundred different solar, wave, wind and hydro-electric power plants by satellite from his office.

Every now and again, especially on misty days, Alice felt sure she caught a glimpse of the black edges of the C-Bean appearing in the distance. But whenever she ran towards it, there was nothing there. One day she found what she thought was Dr Foster's fluorescent string from his penknife. She showed it to Charlie but it meant nothing to him. She must have asked Charlie a hundred times where he put the Mark 3 cardkey but he always said, 'Alice I keep telling you: I don't know what you're talking about.'

Over the years Alice stopped asking questions, and even her memories of the C-Bean and everything that had happened seemed to fade.

One sunny December morning just after Christmas in 2030, Alice was walking along the beach on St Kilda with her family. Kit and her dad were up ahead scouring the tideline beside the crystal clear water for interesting shells and rocks, while Alice and Lori walked arm in arm with their mother.

Alice saw Kit pick something up, show it to his father and then come running towards them, his red hair blowing across his face in the wind.

'Look what I've found Alice, it's just like one of your stories!' In his palm was a thin, flat, black rectangle of metal the size of a credit card.

Alice's heart skipped a beat as she turned it over. On the reverse were the familiar raised letters and the spinning globe logo. She smiled and gave it back to her brother.

'You keep it, Kit. You never know, one day you might need it.' The twelve year old boy tucked the cardkey in his pocket and ran back to his father. Alice sighed and stared out into Village Bay, watching the sunlight sparkling off the sea.

'Mum, do you remember the Christmas I got a seabean in my stocking?' Alice asked.

'Yes, I do. In fact I still have it: didn't you give it to me as a good luck present just before Kit was born? I've no idea what you were so worried about – he turned out just fine!'

They walked back home through the little group of Scots pines on the foreshore. Someone had dug a deep round hole at the edge of the path.

'That must be where we're planting the next tree on New Year's Day,' Lori remarked.

'I forget how beautiful St Kilda is when I'm working in Edinburgh. Why did we come to live here, Mum? Alice asked casually.

'Years before you were born Alice, your Dad read about this amazing place, a world *heritage site on a beautiful island with a unique sustainable community that was miles and miles from anywhere. It sounded wonderful. Then, when Lori was about four and you were still a baby, your Dad heard that one of the cottages here had come available. When we arrived, we were greeted by this kind old man who turned out to be Old Jim. Before we'd even introduced ourselves, he took you in his arms and said 'Welcome home, little Alice' and that's the moment I knew it was the right thing to do – coming to live here. It was as if Jim had met you before in another life and remembered you.'*